ALSO BY JEAN BOOTH

Origins of the Supernaturals
Changed

Standalone Novels
Zombie War

Contributing Author
On the Edge of Tomorrow
Tales by the Tree

JEAN BOOTH

CHOICE

An Origins of the Supernaturals Novel

bhc press

Livonia, Michigan

For Mom,
For believing I could.

CHOICE

CHOICE

Published by BHC Press

Library of Congress Control Number: 2017961407

ISBN: 978-1-64397-039-4 (Hardcover)
ISBN: 978-1-947727-16-8 (Softcover)
Also available in Ebook

For information, write:
BHC Press
885 Penniman #5505
Plymouth, MI 48170

Visit the publisher:
www.bhcpress.com

1

"Once upon a time there lived a beautiful young girl named… Claudia."

Ashlyn made a very inelegant snort. I'd forgotten there was a girl in her class she didn't like that was named Claudia. I gave her a pointed look. Our rule was, if she wanted a made-up story, she wasn't allowed to interrupt. She gave me innocent eyes, lifting one shoulder and pretending to twist a key on her lips, so I continued.

"Claudia dreamed of a happily ever after. She believed the fairy tales she'd read, and every night wished upon a star for her prince to rescue her from the evil witch that was her captor. The years went by and Claudia developed into a striking young woman. She didn't recognize her own beauty, though. She'd spent too many years being bullied by the evil hag that was the only family she'd ever known. Still, Claudia hoped, wished, and prayed for her dashing prince and her happily ever after. Eventually, the evil hag departed from this world, and Claudia was left all alone. Claudia left the only home she'd ever known to seek out other people, hoping to one day find her handsome prince.

"She walked for days in a seemingly endless forest until she could no longer take another step. Curling up against an old oak tree, she prepared for her final sleep. For the first time in her life, she felt true bitterness as she gazed up at the stars. She couldn't understand why the girls in her stories got their happily ever after, while she was destined to die alone after living a secluded, miserable life. She cried herself to sleep that night.

"The next morning, Claudia awoke with a start. In place of the gnarled roots of the old oak tree, a down pillow cradled her head. She opened her eyes and took in the room around her. Directly to her right sat the most handsome man she had ever seen. As soon as their eyes met, they fell in love. And, as in any good fairy tale, they married and lived happily ever after."

"Aunt Tash?"

"Yes, Ashlyn?" I said with a suppressed smile. I knew what she was going to say before the words even left her lips.

"Your stories really stink. You missed out on all the adventure of the prince rescuing the princess from something really bad. Can you try again?" Her big blue eyes pleaded with me. It was our last night together before I left on my vacation, and I knew we were both feeling the sting of the imminent loss.

"Well, quit asking me to tell them if I'm so bad at it," I replied with a chuckle. "I lost my ability to tell stories long before you were born. If you want to read one of your stories before bed, you can go ahead. I'll try to have a better story for you when I get back, okay? I love you very much." I kissed her forehead as I tucked her under her princess sheets.

"Love you, too. Night." She yawned, revealing the gaps in her mouth left by teeth that still hadn't filled in. She was snoring softly before I reached the doorway.

I closed her door so that only a crack of light showed through. She was still young enough to be afraid of the dark, but old enough to think that a night-light was for babies. I made my way to my room to make sure I was all packed for my trip. I didn't live with Katie and Ashlyn, but for the three days that Katie was at work, I stayed with them. It was easier on them, and allowed me to develop a closer bond with Ash than I would have if I only saw her on occasion.

I couldn't help but wonder again, as I had many times before, why little girls treasured fantasy stories so much. How did girls in today's society still grow up hoping for the elusive happily ever after? After everything, why was I still hoping for it?

As I finished up packing, I mentally went over the story I'd told Ashlyn. The portrayal of ugly, disfigured women as witches or shape-shifters that are evil incarnate was not an idea I wanted to promote. It caused girls to believe that beauty is the most important thing to possess. According to stories like the one I'd told Ashlyn, it doesn't matter if a woman is smart, strong, rich, or powerful; if she's not beautiful in society's eyes, she's destined to live life as an ugly, lonely old hag. Part of me regretted telling my sweet niece these stories. Another part of me yearned to keep Ashlyn young and innocent for as long as possible, believing that one day her prince *would* come and rescue her. Her mother and I knew better.

I hadn't been on a vacation since before our parents died. Even when they'd been alive, we'd gone as a whole family. This was my first solo trip. Hell, it was my first solo anything. The nerves tied my stomach in knots and I knew I wouldn't sleep tonight. Grabbing one of my photo albums, I went downstairs to grab a glass of wine and relax.

This book was filled with pictures of Ash, as most of the albums in this house were. I flipped the page until I came to a rare photo in which she was smiling. More often than not she was pulling faces at the camera. God, I loved her.

"Hey, what are you looking at?" Katie's whispered words interrupted my reminiscing.

"Oh, God! You scared the crap out of me. What are you doing back so early?" I said. I picked up the album that had slipped from my grasp.

"Sorry." She smirked. "We were actually overstaffed tonight, and since everyone knows you're leaving tomorrow they let me go home early. How are you doing?"

I shrugged. "I don't know. A part of me is so excited I wish I were on the plane now. A bigger part is terrified. We've never really been apart."

"I know what you mean. I'm so excited for you—this is a trip you've been dreaming about for as long as I can remember. But I also want to be selfish and keep you here with Ash and me forever. It'll be weird not having you around for every little thing. Ash is going to drive me bonkers." She settled herself on the other end of the couch so we could whisper-talk without waking the little monster.

"I thought it would be hard when you married Alex, and I was with Keith, but we've never gone a day without speaking to one another. I wish you would come with me. You know I'd have more fun with you and Ash there."

"No. Tash, this is for you. You need to discover who you are without us. It's important that you do things for yourself—and maybe try to create a family of your own."

I glared at her. This was a conversation we'd had repeatedly. "You know how I feel about that, Katie."

"At some point, you have to let him go. I know Keith hurt you, but there are other men out there."

"He didn't just hurt me, Katie. He destroyed any ounce of desire I had for a marriage, any belief I had that there was such a thing as a soul mate. Disappearing two weeks before our wedding? What kind of messed-up shit is that? Don't give me that look, she's asleep, she didn't hear me swear." I glared at her, knowing where this conversation was headed, and secretly glad for the distraction from my traveling nerves. "Relationships aren't worth the heartache. You think everything is fine, then *bam*! He leaves. No notice, no warning, no excuse. Just gone. And I think I'd have been okay, had he not gotten married so quickly after." I needed to stop, or I was going to start yelling. Even after all these years, talking about Keith made my blood boil. "And then, every freaking time I run into him, the butterflies start right back up, like I'm a hormonal twelve year old, with an insane need for him to notice me. All I want to do is scream at him, make him feel the same way he made me feel, but instead I end up making pleasant conversation and wishing him well. It's been years! I should hate him. I should, but I don't. Truth be told, if he knocked on our door right now and asked me to give him another try, I don't think I could say no. It's been eight years, Katie. I hate being so pathetic."

"He was a jerk. There's no denying that. And you're not pathetic. There are other people out there, Tash. Don't let him define your future happiness. I believe you'll get married one day." Katie gave me a hesitant smile.

"I don't know how you can stay so positive after how things ended with Alex."

"Tash…" Katie sighed.

"Convincing you to have a baby when you specifically told him you didn't want children? Then leaving you while you were pregnant? He was an asshole and you know it."

"He did what he felt was necessary for him. I wouldn't change a second of it; Ashlyn was worth every moment of pain, physical and emotional. I know I didn't want kids, but she makes me wish I had more." Katie's eyes were fixed on her lap, her voice thick. Katie had never forced her ex to have a relationship with Ashlyn, and he certainly never requested custody or visitation rights. It was one of the quickest, most amicable divorces I'd ever seen.

"How can you seriously expect me to believe in happily ever after with everything we've been through?"

"I believe there's someone for everyone. I still believe Ash's father will play a part in her life when it's time. In the meantime, I try to enjoy my life with you and her. I've started doing things for myself again, too. I've been going out with friends while she's in school, and getting back in touch with the things I used to do before I even married Alex. It's nice to know that I still have a personality outside of being a mom and a nurse."

"I do love work, and my bike." I grinned at her, and she rolled her eyes. Shortly after my hell-year, as I liked to call it, I'd gotten a motorcycle. It was fast, sleek, and made for trouble. It had been one of the only things apart from Katie and Ash to truly bring me joy.

I had dreaded the moments in between work and watching Ashlyn. My bike gave me a reason to get out of my empty apartment. I had always been able to lose myself in my job, too. Katie had gone into the side of healthcare that dealt with people, I ran straight to the beakers. Her side dealt with the emotional and spiritual side of healing, whereas mine dealt with the tangible, thought provoking, results-oriented side of healing.

"What kind of science fiction are you cooking up in your lab now? And will it cause us to flee to a hotel again?"

"That only happened once, and you know it wasn't my fault." A few years ago, one of the lab assistants had monkey-napped one of the monkeys we were testing on. He was a member of one of the animal activist groups and we didn't realize it until it was too late. He'd leaked our personal information to the activists and released all the animals throughout the building. It was chaos. When the group realized I was heading the research, they started harassing me at home. They had thrown rotten fruit at my windows, and had even spray-painted my car with vulgar expletives, all in the name of getting me to halt research. It got so bad, I was worried about them finding out where Ash and Katie lived, too. I had asked them to stay at a hotel for a few weeks, until things calmed down again.

"Security has gotten a lot better since that happened. And it was just some rotten fruit and spray paint. Not a big deal at all."

"Right."

"We have some new medications we're testing. If all goes well, it should revolutionize the way we treat people. Genetically specific medications, isn't that crazy?" I knew she could appreciate this, it had been my passion since graduation, and I was finally able to start working on it. "It's another reason I'm having doubts about this vacation. We finally have the green light from our boss, and I'm leaving. We've been isolating different codes to see how manipulations affect the specimen. In another decade or so, we should have genetically specific treatments for patients suffering from anything from cancer to the common cold. It's groundbreaking work, and I'm just supposed to waltz off in the middle of it?"

"It sounds great, Tash, but it also kind of freaks me out. I am glad it makes you happy though." She yawned. "You'd think it'd be easy for me to stay up all night, every night, being a night nurse. As soon as I get home, though, I'm done. You should try to get some sleep, too."

I nodded absentmindedly. I wasn't going to sleep tonight, and we both knew it. I would, however, enjoy a nice, hot bath. I slowly uncoiled myself from the couch and stretched. A bath would be wonderful. I'd always loved the water. I found it unbelievably soothing. It was a wonder that I lived in the desert.

After my bath, I stretched out on my bed, the warm water had soothed my muscles, and despite my nerves, I drifted off to sleep. I'd had a recurring dream since I was a child about a strange land where people shimmered as though their skin was lit by something within. It was similar to the bioluminescence that deep-sea creatures have—an evolutionary trait that lures prey into a false sense of security before death. Everyone in my dream is beautiful, with their slight, simple glow. I'm never a part of the dream, always an observer.

Each time I'd had the dream it was the same. I'd feel myself drifting off, and suddenly I'd be standing next to a table in a large room. There are always many people walking around, giving the table I stand near a wide berth. Seated alone at that table is a man with long, inky hair, hunched over. He's engrossed with what he's working on, and never looks up. I walk around that table, trying to figure out what he's working on, or to see his face, but all I ever see is the top of his head. Then I wake up.

THE NEXT morning Katie and Ashlyn walked into the kitchen as I was making breakfast.

"You ready for your trip, Tash? I still can't believe I'm going to miss your 30th birthday." Katie combed her fingers through her hair. "You need this though, and I'm so excited for you."

"I think so, but I want to check my stuff again. I feel uneasy, like I'm forgetting something. Are you sure you guys will be okay while I'm gone?" I handed her a plate of egg whites, wheat toast, and organic OJ. She was such a health nut.

"I'm sure you have everything. You've been packed for days now. And stop worrying! We'll be fine. Have fun!" She smiled and kissed Ashlyn on the forehead. "Hey pumpkin, eat up so we can take Aunt Tash to the airport. I don't want you any later for school than we're already going to be. What did you two get up to last night while I was at work?"

"Auntie Tasha made up a really lame fairy tale and told it to me. But we had cookie sandwiches and they were so yummy that they made up for the bad story," Ashlyn explained.

"Ash, you stinker! That was supposed to be our secret." I stuck my tongue out at her and crossed my eyes, she giggled.

"I hope you left some for me. You make the best cookie sandwiches. What time is it?" Katie glanced at her watch. "Crap. Ashlyn, go brush your teeth. Tash, do you need help putting your bags in the car?"

My sister and I are so anal retentive, we made it to the airport with plenty of time to check my bags, and make it to the security gate. Somehow, we managed to do it all without crying. I gave Katie and Ashlyn both hugs when they dropped me off and felt a mix of sadness and exhilaration. I wiped a tear away from Ashlyn's cheek.

"None of that, I'll be back in one week. I'm going to miss you both so much, but I'll call when I arrive in Miami." I kissed Ashlyn one more time and made my way to the line through security. They both kept up waving until I rounded a corner, and they were out of sight. I fought against a lump in my throat as I once again wished I'd convinced Katie and Ash to come with me. It was going to be very hard to be away from them, but deep down, I knew Katie was right. I needed to do something for myself. I hadn't left their side since Ashlyn was born. It was past time I find some independence.

Once I was settled in my seat, I watched couple after couple march onto the plane as I sipped my glass of wine. I may have had to pay three times the usual price of a plane ticket for first class, but the perks were nice. It took three glasses before I decided I didn't want to jump out of the plane. I was grateful that the seat next to me remained empty as the plane filled up so I didn't have to endure an awkward conversation with some stranger, or even worse, have some strange person's head on my shoulder.

Flying does weird things to people. One woman spent the better part of a minute trying desperately to shove her oversized bag into an already full bin, going so far as to move other people's things—even though the flight attendant was trying to get her attention. I was glad that my carry-on consisted of the backpack that was stowed securely between my legs. I'd have gotten annoyed if it was my luggage she was being so disrespectful toward. On a plane, there seems to be this unwritten rule that you can't get mad. Boundaries that are normally there seem to slip away as soon as your foot hits the entrance.

I slipped my headphones on and looked out the window as the plane took off. I loved watching everything turn microscopic. Seeing the cars inch by like ants made me feel a childlike delight, like change was in the air. I smiled and leaned back, reflecting on my life. Mostly, I thought about where I'd be if I'd made different choices in my life and if I'd still be so content.

2

I made it to Miami without incident, called home, and decided to get a drink before leaving the airport to check into the hotel.

"You are like a red, red rose, and I'm a little thorny." The familiar words were whispered against my cheek and I was overwhelmed with the smell of mint gum and spicy aftershave. I'd know that scent anywhere. Couple it with the husky timbre of his voice, and my stomach was somewhere in the vicinity of my shoes.

"Keith! Oh my gosh! What're you doing here?" I felt my cheeks redden as I slid off the stool to give him a hug. I inhaled his scent as I was pressed against his chest, and frowned. After everything, I still felt a rush of attraction every time I saw him. Hormones are nasty, deceitful things.

"Hey, babe. Been a long time. I thought I saw you walking in here. Of all the places we could run into each other—crazy." He grinned at me mischievously as he shook his head in disbelief. "The guys dragged me here to pick up chicks." He gestured out the tall windows at the palm trees waving in the breeze. "I got divorced again last year, and haven't really been out since. The boys were kind enough to force me to go on vacation." His face scrunched up, revealing that he didn't really see their actions as a kindness.

"Really? I think you were getting divorced the last time I heard about you. You've got to quit picking the wrong ones." I smiled and shook my head. My heart was resuming its normal cadence in my chest.

"I should've never let you get away." He looked at me with his dark blue eyes and the past eight years disappeared. I was in trouble. I must have blushed, gaped, or drooled, because he started laughing. "Oh, Tasha, you should see your face! I was just teasing, babe. Kind of. What've you been up to?" He asked, flashing his trademark dimples.

I melted, silently vowing to find a way to eliminate the emotional response hormones brought about in the body as my next project.

"Oh, you know, a little of this, a little of that. Katie's daughter is eight, and I get to spoil her every chance I get. I'm a Biomedical Engineer at Double Helix now, so I finally get to play with DNA and mess with the primates." I grinned at him, easily reverting to our old, comfortable conversations. "I'm here celebrating my birthday. I've always wanted to see Bermuda, and this was as good an excuse as any."

"Of course, I almost forgot it was your birthday." He lied easily, but I still caught it. "You're going on that cruise too? We'll have to have dinner tomorrow. We should be in Bimini by then, and I've been told that they have great clubs. You still dance?" His eyes sparkled with the same mischief I remembered from years ago, causing my heart to do another rebellious flip.

"Sure. I could use the distraction. It was so good to see you. Hopefully we'll get to hang out after dinner, too." I cringed inwardly. *Did I really just say that out loud? Way to go Tash, show him how desperate you are for his attention.*

"God, I've missed you." He put his hand on my arm and I shivered. "Shit, my friends are looking for me. I'll see you tomorrow for dinner, then maybe we can get drinks and hang by the pool. I am so glad I ran into you." Before I could reply, he leaned in, gave my cheek a quick kiss, and ran off. I finally realized why I'd had an uneasy feeling about this trip.

I couldn't believe he was here. Despite my best efforts to resist my initial reaction to him, I couldn't help but feel more relaxed with him around. That had been the whole reason we'd been attracted to each other to begin with, I provided him with stability, and he encouraged me to relax. He had been in the middle of a very messy divorce and neither one of us was prepared for the onslaught of emotions that had slammed into us.

We dated for a year before he proposed, and things went downhill from there. His divorce had lagged on due to custody disagreements and he finally agreed to a paternity test so that he could get custody of their son. It came back that he wasn't the father, and it broke something in him. That was the beginning of the end of us. He loved his son more than anything, and was crushed to find out that he wasn't biologically his. He turned to the bottle for comfort. We were working things out, and I tried to give him space to deal with what his ex-wife had done to him. It was never really the same after that, though. The writing had been on the wall for a while, but it still crushed me.

A part of me was glad to have escaped the noose of marriage, though a larger part was heartbroken. He was the first man I'd ever pictured myself creating a family with. I sat nursing my drink, attempting to find meaning in our sudden encounter. I thought of the conversation I'd had with Katie just last night, and suppressed a snort. Of course I'd run into him and have my entire world shift again. Slamming the remainder of my drink, I decided to ignore the whole occurrence and enjoy my first experience of Miami. I wasn't going to let the ex-love of my life ruin my vacation. This trip was all about me, not about rekindling a lost love.

My hotel was a few blocks from the pier that I was departing from, but close enough to downtown Miami that I'd be able to enjoy the nightlife before departing on the ship tomorrow. I managed to book the same corner-room for tonight as I would have for the two nights after we returned. It had an amazing view of the Miami city strip along one wall, and along the adjoining wall the curtains were open, revealing the dark Atlantic Ocean. The vast blackness after nothing but lights was eerie.

I quickly changed into comfortable jeans and a deep red halter-top. I checked out the results in the oversized bathroom mirror, making sure that I looked presentable. I had been dying my hair a dark auburn for a while now, and the ends curled up just above my elbows. My dark brown eyes looked black against my pale skin. My breasts poured out of the halter, displaying my cleavage in the best light.

Katie had always been athletic and toned, while I was referred to as healthy. Whatever people meant by 'healthy' I didn't really care—I took it as a compliment. I turned side-on to the mirror, examining my protruding breasts. Sometimes I wondered if I would be considered athletic, too, without such a large chest. Alas, the boobs blocked the rest of me. I quickly touched up my make-up, and walked out the door with my head held high.

I had always thought of my hometown as being a haven for someone single, but I'd never been to Miami. The strip was lit up with signs advertising bars and clubs, all offering girls free drinks until various times. I assumed this was an unspoken way of encouraging men to gather for the promise of drunken sex. I could already tell this was my kind of town. I took a few minutes to enjoy the scenery before I chose my destination.

Krypt Keeper sounded like a fun club to go to, and my curiosity got the best of me. Stepping around a group of people who were stumbling down the sidewalk, I made my way in the direction the sign pointed. Sure enough, when I finally got past the ID check, there were goths and vamps flooding the place. A Zombie, B-Positive, and Bloody Mary's were the obvious drink options, but the most intriguing to me was a drink called Dracula's Vein; it had vodka, cranberry, and a secret mix that infused a spice I'd never tasted before to the alcohol.

The music was loud; dance with a techno under-beat. I was in my own personal heaven. I was sitting at the bar enjoying my second drink when I saw Keith walk through the door. My pulse quickened and I had to close my eyes to bring it back under control. He was with all his old friends and was the most breathtaking of them all. He was six foot two with short dark brown hair, deep blue eyes, and a body that was honed to perfection from working construction. He was, unfortunately, still able to make my body melt and burn all at once.

"Vaht is a luvley voman like you doing here unaccompanied?" A perfect Dracula wannabe had found his way to me. Great.

I thought I was playing unapproachable bitch better than that, but unfortunately not. I was also hoping that Keith wouldn't see me getting hit on by a dork. I had to have more appeal than that.

"Look, Vlad, is it? I'm flattered that you decided to come over and talk to me, but I'm just not interested in anything right now. Thanks, though." I gave him my best toothy smile that could never be mistaken for anything more than a grimace, and turned away, barely giving him a cursory glance.

"You wound me, darling." He'd dropped the accent. "It's Stephan, not Vlad, and you were starting to look rather lonely sitting here all by yourself. I thought I would buy you another drink or see if you would like to dance." He had silver eyes, and they were fixed intently on my own. I found myself unable to look away. His eyes were mesmerizing, as though someone had poured magnesium into his irises.

He was about a foot taller than my five-foot-five frame, thin but not anorexic looking, with the paleness of a Spaniard who avoided the sun. He wore a deep burgundy shirt tucked into black slacks. His shirt was rolled up to perfectly display toned forearms. I found myself surprisingly attracted to him, although he was paler than I was used to. I looked back up to his face and he was smiling. Definitely a vamp wannabe with his fake incisors, but what a smile.

"My dear, I don't think I have ever been so thoroughly checked out before." He was holding back the laughter that danced in his silver eyes.

"You have amazing eyes," I blurted, my cheeks flushing instantly. "I'm sure you get that a lot, sorry. I don't usually dance; I tend to flail about a bit too much. If you're willing to risk it, I'll take you up on your offer, though." I felt butterflies in my stomach as he grabbed my hand and led me to the floor.

Part of the reason I'd agreed to dance with him was because he appeared to be the sort of guy who was used to tripping over his own large feet. Much to my surprise, we glided to the center of the dance floor without a hitch. People parted very subtly for him without a word between them. We started dancing, moving together as if we'd been doing so our entire lives.

I was never given the opportunity to get nervous. Making eye contact with him, I sashayed to the bass. His hands slipped slowly against my hips—a firm, but gentle touch edging me on. A touch of pressure against my hip, and I spun in his arms. He pulled me close, my back against his chest. He mimicked my hip rolling, and my heart raced. He clutched my hand and I dipped down to the floor before writhing slowly up his body until I was in his arms again.

The music changed and I was an instrument to be strummed. He spun me around, caressing my lower back, grazing the area just above my ass. Shivers spiraled down my body. He tipped me back, bending me almost in half as I rode his thigh. I was on a high I'd never felt, my inhibitions were falling away and I was completely in the moment with this man, this stranger. The hand he used to tip me trailed a path of flames down my arm. He laced his fingers with mine and abruptly brought me up so we were once again staring into each other's eyes.

The beat shifted again, and I lit up as I recognized it. I wriggled out of his grasp so I could jump up and down, thrashing my hair between raised arms. He laughed at me, and we began to do the robot, oblivious to our surroundings. We danced to four more songs before I practically collapsed in his arms.

"I have to get some water, join me?"

"Of course," he said. He led me to a small table in a room adjoining the dance floor. It was dark, and the music was a muffled beat in here. The table had a little reserved sign on it.

"I don't think we can sit here," I objected as I collapsed into the booth.

He smiled and slid in next to me. Without needing to be summoned, a waiter appeared at my elbow.

"What can I get you two?" He asked. I was too busy trying to catch my breath to take proper notice of him.

"A tall glass of water for the lady and the usual for me. Thank you, George."

"Come here often, I see."

His mouth turned up at the corners. "I'm here every night to make sure my patrons have a nice time."

"Your patrons? You mean you own this place?" I blushed as I heard what I'd said, humiliated that I could be so rude. "I mean, you just don't seem the type to be a club owner. You look like you would fit in better in the lab. As a worker, I mean, not…not that you look like a lab geek…I mean guy. I work in a lab, and I'm so going to shut up now. Great club, by the way." My cheeks were on fire.

"No, you are absolutely correct. I am not at all the typical bar owner, but I must tell you it is so much more fun than sitting behind a desk all day. It is rewarding to be able to help people relax, unwind, and enjoy themselves after a difficult day. I am able to sit back and enjoy the scenery while people do what it is that makes them happy. This bar was created to be non-threatening, and violence is not tolerated. I have yet to have the police visit my establishment, and I've been open fifteen years," he explained with an air of pride.

"Wow. That's very impressive. They're thinking of passing a new law back home that after a certain number of visits from the cops, bar owners have to pay a huge fine every time the police are called." I was taken aback that he had owned this place for so long, he didn't seem any older than me. We sipped our drinks for a few minutes, enjoying each other's company. Before too long, he was called away to help at the bar. His drink was a very deep red color, he drained it before standing up to leave, and took the glass away with him. I stayed for a few more songs, and then made my way over to the bar to say goodbye to Stephan.

"You are leaving so soon?" Although he'd dropped the Dracula act, he did still have an accent I couldn't quite place, and a glint of mischief in his eyes. I couldn't help but smile back at him.

"Yeah, I have an early departure tomorrow. I'm going to Bermuda, but will stop by and say hi when I get back. It should be in about a week. I had loads of fun tonight, and am glad that I was able to meet you."

"As am I. Allow me to escort you to your hotel. The Miami streets can be unpleasant at times, and I would feel poorly if something were to happen to you."

His hand was entwined in mine before I had a chance to accept or deny his offer. We walked the block back to my hotel hand-in-hand. I was uncharacteristically nervous with Stephan, yet at the same time I felt very safe.

"Thanks for walking with me. You really don't have to; my hotel is just down the street. Maybe we could get together when I get back, if you aren't too busy with your club?" I asked, more nervous than I'd been in years. It was as if all my experience with casual flings flew out the window. For some reason, I didn't want a fling with Stephan; at least, not *just* that.

"That would be fun. You can reach me there, I have an apartment above the club and am either there or down below."

"That's convenient. We're here. I told you it wouldn't be far." I paused, not wanting to say goodbye to him. "I had fun tonight, it was great meeting you." I wanted to kiss him, but didn't want to seem like a tramp. It was stupid really, as I'd probably never see him again, and I was accustomed to just taking what I wanted from men.

"Natasha, I hope we do meet again, but if my instincts are correct and you are given a choice, I do not think we shall ever see one another. I do so hope to be wrong about this." He leaned down and kissed me. It was startling and tentative at first, but as he started to pull away I held him closer. The kiss deepened and quickly became impassioned. His hands slid up my back, one pulling me closer, and the other fisting in my hair. I could feel his reaction to me pressing tightly to my belly, and felt my knees go weak. He nibbled my ear and then began kissing lower down my neck. I could hear myself moaning and only vaguely wished we weren't on the streets of downtown Miami.

The hand in my hair tipped my head back, and I realized that the hand on my back had slid forward to find my breast. I was whimpering now, a molten body of need when I felt him bite my neck. It was a normal bite that would leave a hickey, but I exploded. It was over in seconds, and I could feel him trembling with need.

"Forgive me; I have taken liberties without your consent. You are an amazing woman, and I do hope to see more of you. Goodnight, Lady Natasha. May the gods bless you with clear skies and strong winds at your back."

I blinked and he was gone. I don't know how I made it to my room, but I was in bed within minutes. It took me until I was almost asleep to realize that I'd never told Stephan what my name was.

3

I took a cab to the ship and arrived just as people were starting to board. Considering I'd only had a few hours of sleep, I felt oddly refreshed. I was also profoundly relieved to discover that Stephan hadn't left a mark on my neck. The ship came into view and I squealed as the cab driver slowed, honking and yelling at the people milling about. Bouncing in my seat, I leaned my head out the window to get a better look at the first ship I would ever be on. It was so big; it was hard to believe it could float. My cab driver was forced to interrupt my excitement at seeing the boat to remind me to pay him.

I boarded and found my room with little difficulty and again was glad that I spent the extra for the suite. It had a window that overlooked the ocean and was toward the bow of the ship, no looking back for me. The towel on my bed was folded to look like a pair of bears. For a moment I missed Ash so much it hurt—she would've loved them. I took a picture for her and reminded myself to get a picture of Stephan when I got back to Miami so I could show Katie. I hurried up to the main deck and waved to the strangers on the pier, pretending they were all here to see me off.

I hadn't realized how high the ship was off the water until I stood at the railing, looking down at the waves lapping against the side. It was unnerving. Once we were well on our way, I wandered around the different decks. The chlorinated pools on two different levels seemed insignificant with the ocean surrounding us. There was a 24-hour workout room with instructors for the day classes. That was probably the most pointless room on this ship—this was a vacation, right? The kitchen, main dining room, and one ballroom were close together, and there were other places to eat on two levels of the ship interspersed with clubs and fitness centers. I made a mental note every time I saw somewhere serving food, or a place providing entertainment.

Walking up a short flight of stairs, I walked around my favorite deck—it had a pool, was open to the sky, and held lots of places to lounge, sunbathe, and even play shuffleboard. I decided to go back to my room, grab my suit and towel, and sit by the pool.

I was a tad irritated to discover that this was not the singles cruise that I was hoping for, but that there were people on their honeymoon and lots of other couples being disgustingly romantic. I wanted to hurl, and not from the waves. I had to remind myself that I was happy and that having a man in my life did not define me. I was going diving in the Bermuda Triangle in a few days, living my life more fully than I could have with a man dragging me down. If I continued to tell myself this, one day maybe I'd believe it.

Top on my priority list was figuring out when the scuba instructors would be doing their lessons so I could take a refresher course. I'd become certified for this trip about a year ago, and had been diving in Lake Tahoe as often as I could. I'd been meaning to explore other lakes because Tahoe is so cold, but it's also extremely clear. I'd bought my equipment six months ago before I'd learned that everything was provided on the ship. The only thing standing between the deep blue sea and me was a pile of waivers to sign.

I appeared topside about an hour before dinner and the first night of dancing. Dancing was offered every night in the different clubs on the cruise ship. I was planning on hitting the disco on the lower deck later, less chance of running into unwanted advances. I had also managed to avoid Keith on my explorations of the ship, which was surprisingly disappointing. Jumping into the pool, I did a few laps before enjoying some of the last rays of the day. I was more relaxed than I'd been in years. As I finished my laps, my thoughts crept toward dancing, stifling the thought that it would be really fun to have Stephan with me in the club. His grace really evened out my flailing limbs.

The dinner bell tolled and I knew it was time to get changed and stuff my face. As I surveyed the dining room, I was amazed at the amount of people—and the amount of food. I'm not a fan of seafood and at certain dinners, such as the one for tonight, I had to request special meals. Some dinners were meant for the crew to meet the patrons and these were catered with very specific meals. I put my fork down halfway through my meal, almost uncomfortably full.

"This sure is a great cruise, isn't it?" the bubbly woman sitting next to me asked.

"Sure. It's my first," I replied, smiling back at her.

"Oh! They're the only way to travel in my opinion! All you can eat, lodging, transportation—really, just about everything is covered they're—"

"Donna, I'm sure the girl doesn't need a sales pitch. She's already here. Let her enjoy her time," the bulky guy sitting next to her admonished.

"Oh, Tom." She waived her hand in dismissal and then turned back to me. "We just got married. I know, this was billed as a singles cruise, but I just *had* to see Bimini. And to go to Bermuda and through the triangle? Oh, I just couldn't pass this up!"

"Yeah, I've seen quite a few couples already," I replied, trying not to sound bitter. *I really don't want a relationship. Honest.*

"Well, I've always wanted to go to Bermuda and Tom is just a gem. He surprised me with these tickets as a wedding present. As if I wasn't already the luckiest lady ever!" She gushed some more about her new husband and I glanced away.

My eyes strayed to the blonde across from me. She was rolling her eyes and shaking her head. Her face contorted in what only could be described as disgust. She caught me looking and I smiled. Sighing deeply, she returned to frantically texting on her phone.

"Sugar, you look simply divine," a sultry voice whispered next to me.

I started at the voice and looked at the man sitting to my right. I smiled.

"Really?"

"Honey, all I have to say is if I batted for a different team, Stuart here would be extremely lonely. And with the way you've been fondling that drink—wow! I'm half tempted to try you out." He winked at me, taking my hand in his and kissing the back. "Maurice, and believe me, the pleasure is not all mine."

I laughed. It was clear by the looks Maurice and Stuart were exchanging that neither of them had any interest in anyone other than each other, but Maurice was putting on a good show.

"What are you guys going to do on this trip?" I asked.

"Shopping," Donna exclaimed. "Bermuda has some of the most amazing gems on the planet, and I just adore stones!"

Tom shook his head and rolled his eyes at me. I smiled at the two of them. I'd never seen such an odd couple, except of course the other couple at our table.

"Oh, girl, whatever catches our fancy. We've been on so many of these things we learned a long time ago that the best deals are the last-minute ones. Stuart's been nagging me to go diving, but I'm just not sure. We've been diving in just about every location possible, but the triangle…" Maurice grimaced. "I'm just not sure about that."

"That's amazing! This is my first cruise," I admitted.

"You really have to make it a habit." Maurice glanced at Stuart. "Stuart inherited his grandfather's estate years ago. It's our goal to see every country there is before we turn forty and have nothing left to live for."

"There's life after forty," I responded with a laugh.

"Of course, but by then things start sagging, wrinkles appear, and," Maurice visibly shuddered, "your body starts to fall apart. We plan on experiencing life as much as possible for the next six years. Already I can see myself decaying." He rubbed a hand up and down his arm as if to show me a withered limb.

"I think you have years before you have to worry about those things." Stuart's voice was slow and soothing with a slight hint at an accent. It was completely the opposite of Maurice's quick, excited animation.

The blonde across the table from me glanced up at Stuart's words, her eyes widening slightly before her brows scrunched in what appeared to be concern. It only lasted a moment, but it was strange. She hadn't appeared to be interested in anything going on at our table before then.

"Who's that?" I leaned in toward Maurice so I could whisper in his ear, gesturing toward the blonde.

"Victoria?" He rolled his eyes. "Don't worry about her. She's weird, been watching Stuart all night, until you walked in." He winked.

Victoria had gone back to picking at her meal, but she was still shooting us glances every now and then, as though she somehow knew we were talking about her. I leaned away from Maurice to talk with the rest of the table.

"Well, I'm going on the dive, and I'm really excited. If you haven't decayed too much, it would be fun to have a couple friendly faces out there with me," I said, grinning.

I noticed Keith and his friends about three tables down from us. It was difficult not to notice them—it sounded like they were already drunk and having a blast. His laughter ringing above the rest caused emotions I didn't want to feel. It was a sound I hadn't expected to hear ever again, making me wonder at the coincidence of meeting him here. Seeing him always made me wonder what would have happened if things had been different. It didn't escape my notice that he hadn't made good on the offer to have dinner with me, but I tried not to think about it.

"You clubbing tonight?" Maurice gestured widely with the mimosa in his hand, excitement brimming in his glassy eyes.

"Maybe." I hesitated. "It's kind of been a long day."

"You have to come! It's tradition," he responded with a dejected look in his eyes.

I smiled. "Which one are you going to?"

"The only one worth going to: disco fever baby!" Maurice jumped out of his chair, twirling around to grab Stuart, and together they sauntered out of the dining hall.

After dinner I seriously contemplated going to bed. My day had just been so busy that I was exhausted; although I'd been having so much fun that I wasn't ready for it to end just yet. I decided that you only live once, so took a quick shower and began getting dolled up. I picked a hot pink, sheer short skirt over black short shorts, a black halter-top and my black ballet shoes. I left my long auburn hair to fall down my back, added some make-up to enhance my dark brown eyes, and was good to go. Thankfully I didn't need ID or money; the bartenders were able to charge your room. I didn't need to ruin my look with a purse.

I went down to the disco and saw that Stuart and Maurice had already started dancing. I sat at the bar, ordered a couple of drinks, and enjoyed the show. I'd started on my third when they spotted me. Maurice flagged me down, miming the act of fishing, so I chugged the rest of my drink and went out to ruin their dancing art. I had to admit that where I lacked in dancing, they excelled. Before I knew it, I was completely sweat-soaked and drunk.

Stuart and Maurice were taking a break to make-out in the darkened corner, leaving me to dance alone. It was a good thing I was trashed or I'd have been humiliated. I'd forgotten how much fun it was to just let go. I didn't even jump when I felt hands start to wrap around my waist. Keith pulled me close and I could smell his after-shave. We moved to the music for a while, wrapped in each other's arms and I knew that we were going to do things we shouldn't.

His lips met mine in the kiss of a man that was starved for affection, and my brain shut off. We were two desperate people craving one another's touch like it was the key to survival. He was the only person who could quench this burning desire I suddenly felt. Without giving my addled brain time to argue about the stupidity of what I was about to do, I grabbed his hand and dragged him quite willingly out of the club and into my bedroom where we picked up where we'd left off. His hands groped and roamed up and down my back. He squeezed my body tight against his quivering member and I moaned into his mouth.

"Tasha, I have to tell you it has been a while."

"Shut up." I slammed him against the wall as my fingers tangled in his thick brown hair. His hand cupped my breasts and I moaned again. His clever fingers teased and searched, and I whimpered. That was all the encouragement that he needed. We pulled apart long enough to throw our clothes off and barely made it to the bed three feet away. Our coupling was hard and fast, a release that we were both craving. When it was over, we collapsed, wrapped up in each other's arms and breathing heavily.

I KNEW it was a mistake the minute I woke up. He was in the shower singing some god-awful tune, and I was trying to figure out how to escape. Sure, my hormones did a happy little jig for Keith, but I was definitely not even remotely interested in starting anything with him again. We had a history, and I was well aware of the fact that he didn't deal with rejection well. He came out of the bathroom in a towel looking yummy, and I had to tell my hormones that we were not starting something with him again. He grinned and they ignored me.

"Hey, babe. Good morning. How are you feeling?" He walked over to me and kissed my forehead. He kept up on his workouts, I know because I watched as the water slid down each crevice of his sculpted abs. *Stupid, stupid hormones.*

"Um, Keith, about last night..."

"I know. It was a mistake on both our parts. I was just so glad to see you again, and while I'd love to see where this goes, I know we need to take it slower than that."

"Oh. Ok, then. I'll just be in the shower. I'll see you later." I peeled myself out of bed trying to remind myself that I wasn't hurt, that I didn't want to have a relationship with him, and failing miserably.

While I finished showering, Keith came in to say bye. We'd arrived in Bimini and he was going sightseeing and rock climbing with his friends, but would meet up with me for lunch. He put his hands on either side of my face as I was still bathing and kissed me with wild abandon. His lips tasted of alcohol, mint, and his intoxicating blend of honey. He laughed and gave my shoulder a gentle nudge back into the shower, then walked out the door. I was shaking as I finished my shower. I didn't want this, right?

4

We were spending the day in Bimini; it was our first stop and also my birthday. The small island of Bimini, as I discovered, was filled with shops, bars, clubs, and vacation hotspots. There were signs everywhere boasting of great snorkeling and scuba diving, something I desperately wanted to take them up on. This would be my first ocean dive. It wouldn't be nearly as deep as the dive I was going on tomorrow, but the nerves were already dancing with anticipation in my stomach.

The white sandy beaches and crystal blue water was perfect for the aquatic lover in me. I decided that I'd go snorkeling this morning and dive in the afternoon. We wouldn't be shoving off until tomorrow morning, so I had all day to explore.

I walked along the beach with my snorkel and fins, contemplating where I was in my life. My birthday was always difficult for me. All it brought was another year of pent up frustrations, anger, and heart wrenching loneliness. My parents had passed away a week before I turned eighteen, and before that, they spent most of their time arguing with each other. It was a battle to get custody of Katie, and figure out the insurance settlement after they died, and I'd been trying to keep my remaining family together ever since. This trip was the first thing I'd done for myself since our parents died.

I'd always found the water to be very soothing, and the ocean was no different. I sat on the beach, my feet barely making contact with the waves sweeping the shoreline. As each wave washed up on the shore it released some of my tension; sweeping away my impotent, frustrated anger and the bitterness I was still clinging to from all the loss in my life. The waves washed it all to the depths below. It was past time that I let everything go and lived for myself.

My mind wandered back to Keith without my permission. Images of the night before floated through my head, but I shoved them away. Running into Keith here had really thrown a wrench in my plans. This was supposed to be all about me, what I wanted, rediscovering who I was outside of work and family obligations. I'd always used them as distractions and excuses to not do things, but I couldn't do that anymore. I was determined to figure out what I wanted in life.

I wasn't even sure I wanted a relationship or if it was the constant societal demands that elicited these feelings. I liked my quiet apartment and wasn't sure I wanted to share it with another human. If I was being honest with myself, I still dreamt of finding my soul mate; that childhood fantasy of the perfect person made specifically for me. Most days I felt the chance of finding that one special person in the world were slim to none. As far as I was concerned, you'd have to be pretty lucky to find someone you could actually stand talking to every day for the rest of your life. If you did happen to find that one person, what were the odds that they'd even be available?

During my contemplation I realized that I had picked up a circular stone that was slightly larger than my thumbnail. I looked down to see what I had found and gasped. It was a flat, perfect circle with writing on one side and a carving of a wolf howling next to a crescent moon on the other. The eyes of the wolf were two tiny emeralds and the moon held what looked like diamonds at each tip. The side with writing was very peculiar. It simply said, *amada*. It wasn't a word I'd ever heard of, but was beautiful to read. Surrounding the stone was a thin strip of silver with a loop at the top for a chain. I knew in my heart that someone carved this for a person they loved very much. Apart from the value, the attention to detail was astounding, especially for being on something so small.

I thought about taking it to the police department but couldn't bring myself to part with something so beautiful. It felt wrong somehow, as if I was denying a gift from the sea. For some reason I felt as if I was meant to find it, that it was fate.

"Thank you, I love it," I whispered to the ocean.

I took my pants off, and put the opal in the small pocket of them before setting them on the beach. The pants and my sandals would mark my place so I wouldn't get lost while snorkeling. I walked out to the crystal blue water up to my waist and put on my fins. Clearing out the snorkel, I put it on, and swam around for a while. I saw sea turtles swim by, interrupting the schools of fish. Below, I could see the sea floor littered with seashells, sand dollars, and starfish. I deliberately didn't go out too far or swim in the kelp or the reefs as I was just trying to get used to being in the ocean for the first time. I was attempting to ignore the fact that I was swimming where sharks lived.

I have a deathly fear of sharks. I forced myself to relax and enjoy the scenery that I was sure to miss if I let my paranoia get the best of me. It was beautiful, filled with fish that were unafraid of a lone swimmer in their midst. I could feel my back warming and knew that the suntan lotion was wearing off, so I decided it was time to go to lunch. I found my pants easily enough, swam to them, and left the comfort of the water. It had been one of the most peaceful swims I'd ever had, once I relaxed.

My phone rang just as I returned to the docks to meet Keith.

"Happy Birthday, Auntie Tash! Mommy told me I could call you today but to leave you alone for your trip. Are you having fun? Do you miss me? What'd you get me?" Ash's excited chatter brought me out of the melancholy mood I'd been in all day from reflecting on my past choices.

"Hey, booger, what makes you think I got you something?" I smiled into the phone. "Of course I miss you."

"I'm your favorite niece, so you have to get me something," she replied.

"You're my only niece," I clarified as I always did. "You'll just have to wait and see. How are you? Are you and your mom doing anything fun while I'm gone? Have you been behaving?"

"'Course I have. We're going to have cake today for your birthday. Mom let me pick it out and everything. When are you going to have your cake? Mom said we could eat ours at any time today so we can have cake together, even though you're far away. We went to the movies today and saw *Janice Kansas in Paris*. It was *so* good. Mommy let me wear my wig. Tomorrow we're going to the zoo to pet the bunnies, and Mommy even said we might be able to ride one of the little ponies." She said all of this in one breath, as excited as only an eight year old can be.

"You're too much. It sounds like you're having lots of fun. Eat your cake after dinner, and give your mom a hug for me. I have to get going, but thank you for the call. I'll see you soon, ok? I love you." I had to get off the phone, talking to her reminded me of how much I missed them both and I could feel a knot forming in the back of my throat as I tried to keep the tears at bay.

"Love you too, bye!" she replied, almost as one word, excited to do whatever was calling her attention.

"Bye," I said into the phone, even though she'd gone. I had tears in my eyes and a smile on my face as I shut it, glad that I'd thought to bring it with me. I thought again about how unexpectedly wonderful my life turned out with those two. They both would've loved this trip, but Katie refused to come. She'd said I needed some time away from being a second mom to Ash and that I deserved to spoil myself for once, instead of them.

"Hey, love, how was your walk? Are you ready for lunch and some shopping?" Keith walked up to me as I approached the pier and gave me a hug, leaving his arm curled around my waist. "What's wrong?"

"Nothing, I was just talking to my niece, Ashlyn. I really miss them. She'd have loved this trip." I smiled sadly up at him.

Keith wrapped me in his arms and just held me for a moment. We stood there in silence for a while and just enjoyed the comfort of each other. He brought his hands up my arms, sending shivers across my body and pulled me close so I was looking into his deep blue eyes. It was hard to remember that he'd hurt me, or that a little over eight years had transpired since he left.

"You okay, babe? We'll be back home in a week and you'll be able to show her all your pictures. I can't wait to meet her. She sounds like a great kid. It was nice she called. Why don't we go get her something special? You haven't gotten her a trinket from Bimini yet, have you?" It didn't even seem strange that he'd inserted himself right back into my life. That's how it always was with us. We clicked and without a thought, we naturally gravitated toward being together.

"No, and I wanted to get a chain to put this on." I pulled the stone out of my pocket. "I found it on the beach. Have you ever seen writing like this? I think it's beautiful."

I showed him the opal and as soon as I dropped it in his hand I regretted it. I wanted to snatch it away from him so he wouldn't contaminate it. It was the weirdest feeling of possession, and it took everything I had to simply let him look at it. I watched him inspect it for what felt like the longest minute of my life. My relief at having it back was frightening in its severity.

"Nope, I've never seen anything like this before, but it definitely took skill. I think it's a genuine opal, but I've never seen one so large or carved so intricately before. The stone is too soft for etching; whoever made this is extremely talented. It's beautiful and probably worth a fortune. You said you found it on the beach?" he asked, absentmindedly.

I opened my mouth to answer, but wasn't given the chance. As we were walking along the sidewalk, I felt someone yank on my arm and pull me to a stop. I looked down to find an old woman tugging at my elbow, pulling me toward an alleyway I hadn't noticed as I was walking along the city streets with Keith. She held onto me and stared at me with unseeing eyes. Her cataracts reflected like cat's eyes in the sunlight. She was a full head shorter than I—all wrinkles and bones. My heart pounded in my chest as her long bony fingers dug into my arm hard enough that I knew they'd leave bruises.

"Beware! A choice you make, twin hearts will break; betrayal so deep you cannot weep; a loss re-woken, heart eternally broken. Beware the curse! Choose with your heart. What pain! Beware the curse!"

She screeched, repeating herself and sounding like a loon, but her unseeing eyes bore into mine with a desperation I could feel to my soul. Keith pried her off me, but I barely noticed him. He could've been a gnat for all the attention she paid him. Once Keith had worked her hands off me, she retreated to the alcove she had come from, still muttering for me to be wary. She continued to stare at me as Keith walked me out of the alleyway.

I didn't even realize I was shaking until Keith wrapped his arms around me. He was whispering some nonsense to me, trying to sooth my frazzled nerves. I'd never been the type of person to get spooked easily, but she'd seemed too earnest in her pleas and warnings. I didn't think I'd ever forget how her sightless eyes bored directly into my soul.

Keith held me close, sheltering me in the warmth of his body as we went to find something for Ashlyn. I found a small turtle made of pooka shells that I knew she'd adore. I also found a beautiful sterling silver chain for my amulet, and when I put it on, it fell neatly between my breasts. I thought about getting something for Katie, but couldn't find anything that I thought she'd enjoy. Keith and I went to a small café for lunch, but I found my encounter with the old woman had stifled my appetite.

After lunch, Keith and I walked around the island for a short while, stopping in the various shops scattered about. We wandered out of the touristy areas, preferring to take our own tour down rarely travelled paths to look at all the wildlife milling about. They were everywhere, even in the places tourists frequented. Almost all the creatures were very interested in the humans walking about. They'd go up to them and sniff for food. It was incredible, yet somehow sad at the same time.

Keith decided to join me in an offshore, shallow dive that one of the shops was offering. We saw a few fish, some sea turtles, as well as dirt, water, and bits of coral in the distance. I was more bummed than I let on, as it was about the same environment as back home in Lake Tahoe, minus the turtles and distant coral. I really hoped that the scenery at the dive tomorrow would be better than today's, but it was a nice, peaceful afternoon that almost succeeded in washing away the incident with the old woman.

We arrived back at the ship just in time for dinner. We were still eating at separate tables, but made plans to go swimming afterwards. Dinner was fantastic, with the same company as I'd had the first night. I told the guys what happened with the old woman and they thought that it was awesome.

"Girl, you met a loon!" Maurice's face lit up like a Christmas tree. Apparently, he'd never been accosted.

"Damn, I can't believe we missed out on that." Stuart's sarcastic tone was meant to be teasing and lighthearted, I was still disturbed and shaken by the whole thing.

"Was she in rags?" Maurice was now leaning over his plate, dessert all but forgotten.

"Sort of, she was hunched over with wrinkly skin hanging on her bones. It was all more creepy than awesome. Her eyes were the worst. They were a very bright reflective blue. You could tell she was blind, but it was as if she could see into my soul," I explained, trying to get them to understand my apprehension and the fear I felt simply looking at her.

"Honey, her eyes were bright because of the peyote. Everyone here smokes that shit. She wasn't lookin' into your soul; she was trying to get money for her next fix. You must have looked like an easy mark." Stuart looked at me with sympathy, and I thought a bit of jealousy, but I'm sure I must have mistaken that.

"Well, Keith rescued me from her, but it was just so weird."

"Oh, I just love intrigue and excitement." Maurice was so elated that I was having a hard time being creeped out by the whole thing. In fact, I was starting to feel a bit silly for overreacting like I did. I could feel a slight blush warming my cheeks.

"Have you two decided if you're going diving with me tomorrow?" We were supposed to be at sea on the main ship tomorrow, but I, along with a small group of certified divers, were going to take another ship and dive at the half-way point to Bermuda.

"Shit, girl, after all the fun we missed with you today, of course we're going with you tomorrow. I just hope they have the space. I'm stoked! You're so not allowed to leave our sight again. I'm not missing out on any more fun." Maurice pouted and looked at Stuart for confirmation that they would be going. When Stuart nodded slightly, Maurice lit up with joy. He was too much fun to watch, it seemed as though every thought that went through his head could be read from his face.

"I've never done ocean diving before," I confessed. "All my diving has been in the lake back home."

"A virgin! You mean we get to be there when you break your ocean cherry? No diving compares to the open ocean." Maurice's face cracked into a grin.

"I'm kind of nervous about the sharks. I hope they leave us alone. I really want to explore the wreckages. I have an underwater camera just for this. Do you think we'll be okay?" I was wringing my hands in my napkin and noticed that Victoria, the blonde from yesterday was listening in on our conversation with interest.

Maurice and Stuart looked at each other with the shared intimacy of a life together. I felt a pang of jealousy as they burst out laughing.

"Girl, you've been watching too much television. This will definitely be an eye opener for you. Sharks are more afraid of you than you are of them. We'll be in a large group in an area that has been used many times before; you'll be just fine. Also, you'll be attached to your buddy. There is nothing to worry about." Maurice was still chuckling to himself as they got up and left the table. I ducked to hide the blush that was creeping up my neck.

Victoria continued to stare, until she finally stood up, her expression a mixture of disgust and irritation.

"You are really strange," she said to me with a slight accent I couldn't quite place. "There are worse things to fear than sharks."

I was flabbergasted. It was the first I'd really heard her speak, and she didn't stay long enough to elaborate on her comment. I brushed her off as I got up and went to my room to change, contemplating the dive tomorrow. I prayed that the sharks would stay away. I put on my bathing suit and went to the pool to watch the sunset.

I was still sitting by the pool when Keith found me an hour later.

"I know it isn't a carved opal, but Happy Birthday, Tash." He handed me a small wrapped box. My heart fell into my stomach and I hoped that it wasn't what it looked like.

"Um, Keith, this is...well..." I was so not smooth. He laughed. It was that deep belly laugh that I secretly treasured because he never opened himself up that much to anyone.

"You should see your face. It isn't that. Just open it." Inside was a very dainty bracelet with a crescent moon and star. It was sterling silver with a diamond in the center of the star.

"You remembered," I said with soft surprise. All my life I'd loved the moon. I could sit under the healing lunar light for a lifetime and never tire of it.

"Even if I didn't, all I had to do was watch you at night. You're always so peaceful watching the moon. I've never seen anything so beautiful as you in moonlight." My heart did a nasty little flip and I knew I was headed into dangerous territory.

"I have always loved the water and the moon; they have such a harmonious and symbiotic relationship. It makes me feel as if all is right in the world. This is great, thank you, Keith."

"I love you, Natasha. I think I've always loved you. Seeing you again, being with you—it reminds me of what I lost. What we lost. I'm such an ass, and while I don't expect you to just forgive everything I did to you, I just wanted you to know. I love you. I screwed up before, big time, but I promise to never hurt you like that again." I placed my finger on his lips, leaned forward, and kissed him softly. I felt hopeful for the first time in years. I wanted to fade away into the warmth of this feeling, but there was still something bothering me.

"Keith?"

"Yeah, babe?"

"A long time ago we talked about romantic things, and I never got around to asking you if you believed in soul mates." I asked it quietly, adjusting myself to snuggle against him and watch as the stars started peeking out of the darkening sky.

"I don't think that was a question, but, no, I don't. I think that two people can become compatible with each other for a time, but no, I don't think that my soul was split in half and the other half is lost out there without me. I mean, think about it; with the billions of people on the planet, how are you supposed to find the one that carries the other half of your soul? And on the off chance that you did find that person, who's to say you're even attracted to them, or that they're even available? No, I think that two people, who find themselves attracted to each other, grow and develop a lasting relationship based on mutual respect, understanding, and sex. Yes, I think sex is a very big part of a relationship. If you can't be intimate with the person you love and show them in the most basic of ways that you love them, what's the point? Did I answer your question?"

"Yes."

With us being in port, we had the deck to ourselves. We could hear the waves crashing against the ship, and the far-off sounds of thumping music from the clubs that scattered the piers. It was a little piece of heaven. The silence dragged on, his whispered voice seemed loud when he next spoke.

"Well, are you going to tell me, or do I have to pry it out of you?" His heartbeat sped ever so slightly under my ear.

"I do believe in soul mates. It's one of the few things I still believe in from my childhood. I think that it's our job to find the other half of our soul and connect for a complete life, however long it lasts. Do you think that even if you don't believe in the idea of a soul mate, it can be true anyway?"

"Do you mean could we be soul mates? It's possible. I was rather lost without you, and am happier now than I've been in years."

He held me close in his arms, and I knew at that moment that whatever feelings I thought were returning for him were only from my traitorous hormones. He might be a wonderful man, quite possibly the man that I should settle down with, but he was not my soul mate. If I were to find love and risk my heart again, I'd not risk it for anything less than everything. I wanted more than what my parents had. I wanted a shot at what everyone should have, my soul's other half to share my life with. I fell asleep in Keith's arms watching the stars, thinking about life. He woke me with his light snores a few hours later.

"Keith, wake up. We have to go to bed. We're diving tomorrow and I don't want to miss that." Hand in hand we walked to my room and slept.

5

Morning, lover."

"Ugh, toothbrush. Now." I pulled the covers up to my nose, mostly to hide my grin.

"Now that's just mean. You're supposed to be all mushy when someone loves you."

"Fine, just brush your teeth. You smell like fish." I pulled the covers over my head to hide my smirk. He laughed, dragging me into the bathroom with him.

Forty-five minutes later we were clean, satisfied, and late for breakfast. We grabbed a quick bite and headed to meet with the other divers. I forced my bagel down to settle my nerves, while Keith practically danced around the halls. He was so excited to share this with me and to see some of the wreckages we'd read about. His excitement was contagious.

"Don't worry, Tasha, we're going to be fine. I've been on dozens of ocean dives, and it's just like diving in Tahoe, only better. You're so going to love this! The water is so much warmer than

Tahoe and should be very clear. I won't let anything happen to you, I promise."

"I'll get over it, just let me be." Stupid fear. I wished I'd never seen Bite. Whoever thought great white sharks mauling people and hunting an entire family would make an excellent film was a genius and a sadist in one. I admit it was a great movie, just not for an impressionable seven year old. I'd had a fear of sharks since the first time I saw the girl thrashing about in the shark's maw. *I can do this.* I wanted to do this.

I reminded myself that it'd be just like riding my sport-bike; stupid, reckless, and so much fun. I bought the motorcycle on a dare, not realizing the freedom it'd bring to my life. I was determined since then to live my life to its fullest potential. It was a reminder I needed right now. Nerves and fear are healthy. They help keep you safe. While it wasn't altogether natural for someone to dive, I knew this would be fine. It was as controlled as diving could get.

"Don't let fear rule your life," I whispered. Keith turned and smiled at me. His hair was disheveled and his wet suit fit him like a second skin. A little thrill went through me at the thought of him being mine. My hormones did their happy dance, and I smiled back.

"Are you sure you want to do this? We could just stay in bed all day if you chicken out." He took me in his arms, nipping my nose with his lips.

"Shut up. I'm okay, now. Let's go." I laughed at his antics.

Before the skiff would depart, we had to go through the final instructions from the lead diver, Jorge Mendoza. He was the one directing the more novice divers like me, unless we were partnered with a more experienced diver. Keith had been on dozens of dives, and I knew he'd keep me safe. He and I were with his friends, and Maurice and Stuart were able to join our group. Keith's friends were the same rambunctious guys he used to hang with, the playful ribbing continuing as if time had never separated us.

There were a few other people that I hadn't seen before, and I was especially surprised to see Victoria. She wore the same scowl that I was beginning to think was her customary expression, hidden behind more clothing and sunscreen than I'd ever seen on a young, attractive woman. Jorge was an older guy with an expression of absolute seriousness. He didn't seem too excited to be taking us out in the deep ocean.

"Now, before we take off, there are some rules to follow. Number one: do not let go of your buddy. Number two: keep an eye on your O2 tank. The boat will be out here for approximately three hours, or until the last one of you returns, whichever is first." Jorge's voice was stern, clipped. He didn't wait for us to settle down, rather he expected us to shut our traps and listen. "Remember that time is your enemy down there and that depth can be deceiving. You need to plan for fifteen minute stops every fifty feet you're down to avoid getting the bends. You're all experienced divers or you wouldn't have been given clearance to dive. Remember to be safe down there; I'd like to be able to have a congratulatory dinner with all of you when we get to Bermuda this evening. Be back at the skiff no later than thirteen hundred hours, that's one o'clock for you landlubbers." His eyes met mine for a moment before darting off and continuing.

"If you're not back by then I'll assume you've lied on all your paperwork, or have decided on a nice ocean grave, and we'll leave you there. Your loved ones will be charged for the loss of my equipment, and will be given a letter explaining your stupidity. I notice a few of you have the Neptunic shark suit. Let me assure you that these will not be necessary. We're farther out than the sharks generally like to hunt, and as long as you remain in your group, you should be safe. However, I do appreciate the extra safety measures; it tells me you're paying attention. Let's be safe and have fun, people.

"On a side note, while we have snacks for you on the boat, they are not for the fish. I realize this is rather tempting, but please do not feed the animals that you encounter. The dolphins and sea turtles are curious creatures and will enjoy being pet and fed. Please do not do either of these things as you could disrupt the natural order of life in this area. It does not help to try and domesticate them. Synchronize your watches now. It is currently oh-eight-thirty. You are to be on my deck no later than thirteen hundred or you will be left. Have fun people."

With that, the small boat roared off, taking us miles ahead of the cruise ship. We could barely see Bermuda off in the distance, or Bimini with our docked ship behind us. It was rather eerie to be bobbing about with just glimpses of land and our cruise ship. I knew that wouldn't last though, and by the time we were finished with our dive, the ship would probably be closer to Bermuda than we were.

As we put on our gear, I was happy to note that both Keith and I were wearing the Neptunic shark gear. It was top of the line, and really helped calm my fear of being mauled by sharks. After securing the camera strap to my wrist and my bowie knife on my thigh, I checked Keith's gear and oxygen supply, then turned so he could check mine. I'd forgotten how heavy all the equipment was and couldn't wait to get in the water. We tethered together and at Jorge's signal, went overboard.

My pulse was racing; I focused all my energy on keeping my breathing steady. All I could envision was leaping into the opening maw of a great white. My eyes reflexively closed shut—if I were to get eaten, I certainly didn't want to witness it. Something swam in front of me, I felt a hand caress my face and I opened my eyes to see Keith facing me so that he could make sure I was okay. Seeing that neither of us was shark bait calmed me a bit. He gestured in front of us, encouraging me to take in the beauty I was missing. I was in awe. The Investigating Nature channel couldn't encompass the beauty of what I was witness to.

We were hovering just above reefs filled with coral, seaweed, and wreckages the ocean was slowly working on claiming. Fish of all sizes and colors swam around our little group, investigating the strange visitors to their habitat. Keith and I meandered down toward the reef. Sea turtles swam up to us, head butting us and allowing us to feel the slick algae-covered shells protecting them. It was spectacular. I almost forgot to take pictures for Ashlyn. She'd be in heaven right now.

Next to Janice Kansas, Ash loved dolphins and sea turtles more than anything. As I was filling my memory card up with dozens of photos of the turtles, a pod of dolphins arrived to join the fun. They swam around us, darting close enough to touch, then swimming quickly out of reach.

The reef was awash in colors. Plants and creatures were swaying in the current; fish of all shapes, sizes, and colors swam around us as if we didn't exist. Sea horses darted out from their hiding place of seaweed to play in the bubbles created by our regulators. This was definitely more amazing than the shallow dive we'd had yesterday in Bimini.

We continued to dive to the first of the shipwrecks we could reach safely, and started to explore. The reef had caves with eels slithering in and out. I shivered as we swam by. Sea snakes and eels were on the list of things I never particularly wanted to experience. The shipwrecks started to the side of the reef with coral growing all over. My heart pounded with fear and excitement as we approached the first ship. It was spectacular and looked to be about fifteenth century, completely cleaned out of anything but the iron and wooden fixtures.

I gently brushed my hand across the side, expecting the wood to crumble but it didn't. It was surprisingly sturdy under my palm, slick with algae, covered in bits of reef, but strong. I felt like a mermaid searching for the lost treasure of humans. The ships had holes in their sides; some were completely broken in half. The sun shone through the waves, glittering and sending shadows everywhere amongst the wreckage.

Keith let me explore on my own, but he was always close by to lend a reassuring hand in case I became scared or nervous. His friends were in my peripheral, and Stuart and Maurice were holding hands while they swam. It was one of the most romantic things I had ever seen. I snapped a picture of the two of them.

Keith went ahead of me into the belly of the halved ship, while Stuart and Maurice followed through the first wreck. There was really only space for us to swim in single file, and the water was slightly cooler in the ship, where the sun never entered. I forced myself to stay calm with these three experienced divers. I knew Keith wouldn't lead me into a place that would be trouble. He held a flashlight that seemed to appear out of nowhere. I'd been too preoccupied with myself when we were loading up to see what he'd packed. He illuminated seaweed, shelving, stairs, and some very old frames devoid of the pictures they once held. It was oddly eerie, and the sound of my breaths coming in and out of the regulator weren't helping the macabre environment at all.

Each ship we explored looked similar, the desolation and isolated solitude of them caused a sadness that I didn't expect to fill me. It was akin to walking through a cemetery. I was both disappointed and relieved to note that there weren't any skeletons floating around. Pirates or treasure hunters must have cleaned out the ships years ago. The beauty, destruction, and sense of past adventure was breathtaking.

All too soon we needed to head back to the rendezvous point. Stuart and Maurice were already halfway up, after relating to us that they needed to rise or risk running out of oxygen. At their reminder, we checked our tanks, surprised that they too were almost at the level necessary for us to rise. Keith and I were just getting ready to head to the surface when Keith indicated that he wanted to look at something. He flashed five fingers telling me he needed five minutes and I followed him around the bow of the wreck.

I rounded the wreck we'd just visited and saw a green fin disappear a few more feet below, into the ship's break, just past the mast. It was strange looking, almost like kelp, but shimmery. I pushed past Keith, knowing the distance wasn't going to hinder our return trip to the surface. Curiosity overwhelmed me; I had to know what kind of creature had that strange, thin fin. Just as I was passing the break, I hit a tide. If we weren't tethered and very close to the ship, I'd have been lost. Gripping onto the mast of the ship, I looked up to Keith to indicate that I was done when I saw them. Five hammerhead sharks were circling us, thirty feet above our heads.

All reason escaped me. I panicked and bolted away from them, forgetting about the current I'd just hit. Keith tried to pull me back with the cord and I freaked out even more. I thought the sharks had noticed my panic and were eating him, zeroing in after me for their second course. In my blind fear I grabbed my knife and cut the cord, unwittingly allowing myself to be sucked into the current. I tumbled around the wreckage, hitting the wood and reef with my body and equipment. I saw a glimpse of Keith with what I thought were sharks still swimming above him. I felt my head collide with something, then nothing.

6

I awoke with a start to a pair of teal eyes. I knew I had to be dead because that color didn't exist in nature. The eyes were lined by thick black lashes. He was tan, but his skin was luminous, as though there were a rainbow of colors dancing underneath. His straight, inky black hair fell out of a clip holding it back from his face. The bits I could feel against my skin were like the finest strands of silk. I was afraid to move and see the rest of him, for no man should ever be as beautiful as what I'd seen so far.

"You have woken. Are you in need of anything?" He spoke and my stomach danced with somersaults and acrobatics. His voice was a deep timbre that brushed against me like velvet. My heart skipped a beat and the rest of me was instantly heated. Never in my life had I ever experienced a reaction like that. With two sentences I was utterly lost in him.

"Am I dead?" My voice came out in a throaty whisper. It felt like sandpaper had rubbed my insides raw.

"Do you wish to be so?" he rumbled.

"Not particularly. Who are you? Where am I? What happened?" I tried to sit up so I wouldn't feel so intimate with this stranger, but he placed his hand on my shoulder, preventing any movement. It was as if an electric current went through my body at his touch. His strong arm held me down gently and a soft sigh escaped his lips. If I hadn't known better, I'd have said he was experiencing the same overwhelming feelings that I was.

"Forgive me, my lady. I did not think. You are not dead in the physical sense; however to those outside this place, you are gone. I am called Raifuku. You are located in my bed as I was unable to move you to the Council without harming you. You drowned and were transported here thanks to Poseidon. Are you well?" he asked.

"I drowned?" I again made a move to get up. "Please—let me up."

He bowed his head and I took that as assent. Sure enough, when I sat up and was able to see the entire view of my rescuer, I was not disappointed. He was the most breathtaking creature that had ever walked this earth; an Adonis brought to life. He wore only a pair of dark teal drawstring pants. They were unlike any material I'd ever seen before. It was like staring into the depths of the ocean. My fingers grasped at the fabric of their own volition, and it was as soft as the down feathers of a baby bird. It was by far the most incredible pair of pants I had ever noticed covering a body that should never see a need to be covered. He wore them low on his hips, and I could tell that they were all he was wearing. He had broad shoulders and muscles on top of muscles.

If he wasn't so breathtaking I'd have been terrified of his strength. His entire body shimmered with an ethereal teal blue hue that would normally make me think of rainbow parties back home, but on him it was very masculine. I had never felt petite, vulnerable, or as amazing as I did just sitting on his bed with him sitting beside me. It took me a ridiculous amount of time to realize I was naked. I pulled the sheet over myself and blushed.

"Thank you, Raif, for…everything." The corners of his mouth curved upwards at the nickname I gave him. "How did I end up in your bedroom? How am I not dead?" I could feel my cheeks darken further as my thoughts wandered into dangerous territory.

I knew I should be concerned about my situation, but all I could think about was him. His presence was intoxicating. I was aware of our proximity and the intimacy of our position in an almost obsessive way. Looking at him, I almost forgot the fact that I'd drowned. If he touched me again, I thought I might die for good. My body was molten liquid, only sheer willpower holding me together and keeping me from making a complete fool of myself.

"The current brought you to my doorstep. When the portal opened, you quite literally fell into my lap. I was unsure of what you were exactly, until I was able to remove your extras. I certainly hope that they were unnecessary and not a physical part of you," he said, his brow furrowing. "I would hate to have caused you any unnecessary pain. Thank Poseidon you share our females' anatomy, for reviving you was a simple matter. You have been asleep for some time now. I worried I had removed some vital portion of you so I was leaning over to verify that you still had breath. Are you whole and well, or do you have need of anything?"

He was very animated as he talked. His body and expressions portrayed every ounce of struggle and frustration that he felt. When he was explaining how he was afraid he may have hurt me all I wanted to do was hold him to take away some of the pain and fear in his expression. He was hypnotic and I could have listened to him all day. I struggled to make sense of what he was saying and failed. All that existed was him. I'd never before had such a reaction to anything or anyone. My mind kept envisioning us together with such vivid detail that I could practically feel the imprint of his hands in the most intimate of places.

Raif took away any sense of what should have been important. It was much more important to find out what the hell happened after the sharks scared me than it was to think only of a soft satin sheet and a pair of silky pants blocking what could very well be every fantasy come true.

It was such an odd time to realize that my clothing, as well as all my equipment, was in a pile in the corner of his room. That's when I noticed his room. It was like being inside a seashell. Everything shimmered except the carpet. The carpet looked like rabbit fur. He had a wardrobe made from seashells and a large four-poster bed made from a dark wood I'd never seen before. His sheets were satin smooth and extremely comfortable. They were also the only color in the room, black with teal embroidery. It was a very plain décor, yet it seemed to suit the owner.

"My lady, are you ill? Have I done something incorrectly? Did I—" I placed my fingers on his soft lips, suppressing a shudder as another wave of awareness washed over me. This had to be a side effect of whatever had happened to me. I'd never been so aware of my body in such a sensual way before.

"Raif, I'm fine. I'm just a little overwhelmed at the moment, but doing rather well, all things considered. Can you hand me my clothes? Where are we?"

"My apologies, my lady, I did not see fit for you to continue to wear such archaic clothing and sent to have some made for you. They should be here shortly. We are currently in my bedchamber," he said, bowing his head slightly in respect.

"Thank you, Captain Obvious. Can I at least borrow a pair of pants and a shirt until my clothes get here? I'm uncomfortable being naked in your bedroom. I realize that we're still in your bedchamber as you put it, but what island is it located on exactly, what continent?" I was getting nervous at his refusal to tell me where I was. When I was nervous, I was bitchy.

He moved to his wardrobe with a grace I could only dream of having. His muscles bunched and rippled as he walked away. That man had the best ass I had ever seen.

The sense of loss I felt without him by my side was staggering with its intensity, but I fought against it. I didn't understand my strong reaction to him, but was uncomfortable with the things he was conjuring inside me. In thirty years I'd never instantly craved someone. Even that wasn't a strong enough description, though. It was worse than a craving. The expression, 'love at first sight' popped into my head. I frowned, trying to release such a juvenile notion. People don't really fall in love at the first sight of a pair of teal eyes.

Forget that he was more powerfully built than any other man I had ever seen. Calling him a man even seemed like an insult to him, for no man was nearly so perfect. It was just lust and the after effects of drowning. That thought brought me back to the more important issue at hand. If I'd drowned, how was I still alive?

"I am unsure of the fit of my clothing on your body, but I do have an older tunic that may be small enough for you." He brought the item to me and I noticed that it was also teal. Everything he had was in the greener side of ocean colors. His hand brushed mine as he gave me his shirt and I had to relearn to breathe.

"We are located on the third isle, called Sumner. Not many travel here as the mainland is much more populated and exciting. Sumner is my family's land. We are what you would call farmers. We provide the food for our people and care for the variety of plant and animal life to maintain harmony here. I like the wilderness and the solitude of my life. The quiet is soothing to me and so I chose to stay here instead of residing on the mainland. Never in all my years did I imagine someone like you would fall into my lap. Do you need assistance in your dressing, my lady?" He asked.

"Um, that's probably not a good idea, but thanks. You've avoided my question very well, telling me something while still saying nothing. Where am I, and how soon can I call my family to let them know I'm okay?"

"My lady," he started with a pained expression on his face.

"My name is Natasha. Please call me that or some variety that suits you. 'My lady' just makes me feel old," I said with exasperation.

"As you wish, Natasha." My name was like heaven on his lips. "As I mentioned, you are in my bed, in my bedchamber, in my home on Sumner, which is located in Atlantis, which is approximately eight miles beneath the ocean's surface. We are not detectable by any of your people's modern equipment. We are able to view the surface life, but unable to communicate with any of its inhabitants. Regrettably, you are not able to contact your family, and you cannot go home." The cadence of his words melted me; making me feel safe. It took a moment for the meaning behind his words to fully strike me.

"What do you mean I can't go home? I don't belong here! What have you done to me?" I felt as though he were bewitching me. I clutched the shirt he'd given me close, as if it were a lifeline. The shirt held his smell: a crisp ocean spray during a hurricane, fresh, wild, and untamed. It was very heady and comforting. I realized what I was doing and quickly pulled the shirt over my head.

"Natasha, my lady, forgive me for I do not know how to answer you without offense. I have had minimal dealings with the Surface Dwellers. Certainly none as beautiful as you. Even the ones I've met, I only did so after they'd been to see the Council. The Council will know how to guide you, and they will help you with your answers. We will be going there just as soon as Michael returns with your clothing. I did not wish to take you there in your previous state. Please forgive me." He was kneeling so close to me on the side of the bed that I felt every pore on my body react to his nearness. He leaned in close and reached out, but let his arm drop before he touched me.

I blushed, my abdomen tightened, liquid heated my core, my nipples hardened into little pebbles. He hadn't even been this close to me when he woke me. I felt like I was falling into his teal eyes that shimmered with a heat that mirrored mine. After he'd said I was beautiful, all his words blurred together. He was so close, and we were both tormented by restraint. I couldn't have held back if my life depended on it. Not with him so close and looking so tortured.

I kissed him. Just a slight brush of lips on lips, but I felt it to the very core of my soul. I felt as if I had just come home and for the very first time was whole. Everything changed, yet everything was the same when my lips parted from his.

A knock on the door interrupted my thoughts and he leapt away from me. He looked relived, or confused. I couldn't tell which. "Who calls?"

"It is I, Michael. I have the woman's dress, is she awake? I'd very much like to see her. The whole island is talking about the gift Poseidon sent us. The Council is demanding you bring her to them, conscious or not."

Raif clenched his hands into fists, and closed his eyes for a moment to collect himself. The man really needed to learn how to mask his feelings. I stood up and walked over to him. Timidly, I put my hand on the middle of his back, and as he turned, I hugged him close to me. His chest was solid under my cheek and I could hear his heart beating very fast. He waited a moment, and then I felt his arms engulf my upper body. I felt tiny, and I'd never felt tiny before.

"Are you okay?" I whispered so Michael wouldn't hear us from the other side.

"Why did you…? Yes, I am well. We should let Michael in so you can change."

He released me from his embrace and slowly brought his hand down my arm to entwine his fingers into mine. I could not suppress the shiver that ran down my spine. His other hand opened his bedroom door to reveal a small, skinny man holding fabric of deep teal, darker than Raif's eyes. The man's eyes bulged at the sight of me in Raif's tunic, holding his hand.

He was beautiful in his own way, but didn't have the presence Raif had. He was my height, with ice blond hair, blue eyes, and shiny blue-tan skin. If it weren't iridescent, I'd have thought he had the pallor of a dead surfer. He too wore nothing but pants, but as Raif's were teal, Michael's were the same blue of his eyes. His smaller stature was incredibly muscular as well, but only a third the size of Raif's. He was actually more my type than Raif was; yet I felt nothing compelling about him at all. Next to Raif, Michael was insignificant.

"Hello! I'm Michael. You recovered rather quickly; I was in a coma for about a week before I was introduced. I'm almost sorry to give you this dress; I'd never thought to see anyone in Raifuku's clothing but him. It's rather cute. Do they say cute anymore up there? Sorry, I'm babbling. Raifuku, you'd better get her to the castle quickly. I'll go and alert the Council to your arrival. Nice to meet ya, lady." Michael tossed the dress to me and scurried off. Raif looked back at me reluctantly as he made his way out of the room, finally shutting the door and leaving me as alone as I could be, knowing he was on the other side, waiting.

7

After they left and I was alone in Raif's room, it finally hit me that I was trapped here. Dropping the dress, I ran to the only other door to find it was a bathroom with a window that didn't open. Entering back into the bedroom, I discovered that the windows here were unlocked, but I as much as I wanted to get back home to see my family, I was hesitant to leave Raif. One thing I knew I needed was to get dressed. I couldn't very well escape in nothing but a long shirt. Picking up the dress, I was once again distracted by the texture of the fabric here. It was a softer than silk dress of deep teal, it shimmered ever so slightly in the sun coming in through the windows and was a perfect fit.

After I was clothed, I looked through my belongings for the pouch in my swimsuit that I'd put my necklace in, and put it on. I felt profoundly relieved with it nestled between my breasts again. It was gently tucked under the dress so that no one could see it, but I could feel its comforting weight against my skin. It's strange, the things you find comforting when your world is crashing down around you. The mundane little things seemed to ground me, make me able to process more than the nagging, physical ache I had with wanting to throw the door open and see Raif again.

I wasn't sure how—or even if—I was processing anything, but I went about my methodical way of cleaning, organizing, and identifying everything I had left. Once I located my camera, I quickly took a picture of the room. Suddenly I was struck by the thought that I was still acting as though I'd be able to show Ash all my photos when I got home. But I wouldn't be going home. I was trapped, on an island that shouldn't exist. I'd essentially died to all of my family. I leaned against the wall, my legs suddenly unable to support me.

I started shaking. I'd died. Was I still dead? Was this all some bizarre hallucination? Atlantis isn't real—everyone knows that. It's a myth told by Plato to convince people that a democratic society was perfect—until it wasn't. If this was a dream, or death, it was certainly very real. I slid down the wall and brought my knees to my chest to control the shaking in my body. My heart beat to a steady crescendo behind my breasts that were cleverly contained in this ridiculous dress made for a princess. A scream started deep in my throat. Not one borne of fear, but deeper; the scream of rage. If I gave into it, I knew tears would certainly follow, and I hated showing that much vulnerability to people I liked, let alone to complete strangers.

I could feel him coming before the door slammed opened and Raif barreled in. I didn't think I'd ever understand or be able to explain what it felt like to have someone else inside you. Not in a sexual way, or a maternal way, but as if there was a faint echo of another being inside my very soul. It unnerved me more than the thought of dying or being in a mythical continent ever could.

"What is wrong?" Raif bellowed as he quickly searched the room, a wickedly curved knife in one hand. I realized that the scream I was holding back had morphed into some pathetic keening noise. It was unacceptable. Bolting to my feet, I ran up to him.

"I died!" I screamed back at him. "I fucking died and can't ever see my family again! What the hell am I supposed to do with that?" He stopped his search as if he'd been punched. His knife dropped to the floor and his hands revealed his helplessness, held open by his sides. "How am I supposed to live down here? What about Ash?" I dropped back to the floor, my heart breaking at the thought of my little niece never knowing what happened to her aunt. To never see her face again, never hear her hyena laugh. Visions of things I'd miss with her ran through my head. A weight like none I'd ever felt landed on my heart. Tears poured down my cheeks, sobs wracking my body in great waves of hopeless despair. I was helpless to contain them.

"How can you keep me prisoner here, when we both know I don't belong?" I looked up at Raif, not caring about my heartbreak. "Why can't you just send me back?" He knelt in front of me; anguish contorting his face to mirror the pain of my own.

"I do not know how to fix this. We have had few Surface Dwellers enter our domain, but all seemed more relieved at being here than anything else. You are the first to come to me, and I am not adept at the gentler parts of life. You should have gone to someone else. You deserve better than me." Wrapping me in his arms, he gently caressed my hair.

I closed my eyes, leaning into his touch. As frustrated, scared, and upset as I was, just being with him helped. My tears slowed, the anguish wasn't so much to bear.

"You have to meet with our king and the priest. They have been demanding your presence, but I refused to let anyone see you in your previous state. The thought of others seeing your natural form causes a reaction in me that I do not wholly understand, but am not willing to examine or accept." His jaw and arms were tight as he told me this, as if he were holding onto his anger and jealousy by a thread. I had to admire him in his indignation and was flattered that a complete stranger should have even an ounce of concern about my nudity. I leaned into his chest, his arms relaxing into a gentle embrace. We both sighed. "It is not all bad here. While you did not choose to arrive, I cannot in all honestly say I am disappointed at having you here." I smiled into his chest.

"Thank you, Raif, for being kind." I could feel his whole body melt in my arms. I wasn't sure if it was me, or the electric current zipping through, but surely no one could stay tense with that much stimulation. Just hugging him made me forget everything else in my life. I'd never dreamed that I could love someone so much in such a short time.

Wait.

No.

I don't love him.

I've only known him for an hour! This isn't possible. I can believe that I died, I can even believe in the existence of a mythical island, but this?

No way.

I pulled away before he noticed I was shaking.

"Raif, tell me about Atlantis. If I am going to be stuck here, I'd like to at least know a little about it." I was amazed that my voice hid the trembling I still felt in my limbs. I prayed that whatever was happening to me was just an after effect of dying, or almost dying, or whatever had happened. I prayed fervently that I'd be able to leave this place and return to Katie and Ash where I at least understood my life. I couldn't live without them, and a portion of my heart was starting to believe that I wouldn't be able to live without this man I barely knew. I desperately needed a distraction.

"What would you care to know?" Raif's voice was barely above a whisper, and it was quavering so badly I knew he was having just as much difficulty as I was. A distraction would be good for both of us.

"Anything, everything. How did it come about? What's your culture like? Why'd you sink? Where were you located? I want to know it all." I was pacing his room, slowly distancing myself from him because my entire being wanted to fling myself into his arms and never let go. What was wrong with me? Maybe when I met with the priests they'd tell me that this was some weird Atlantean bond and that when I left, it would too.

"I will tell you the story that is passed down from generation to generation in my family. Our origin is a rather long story, and barring no interruptions, should last as we walk toward the castle. I cannot delay your introductions any further, or I will face the king's wrath. Would that be sufficient for you?" He was so animated, mesmerizing really. I found myself leaning against his plush bed just watching him talk. Every nuance was displayed on his face, his whole body shared in his frustration and love for his homeland. I'd never seen someone so open, so vulnerable, and innocent.

"Okay. Let's go."

I was very careful not to touch him as we left his house. I wasn't sure what would happen anymore. It felt like every time I made contact with him, my heart left to meld with his. Even after just a few casual touches, I felt bereft without him. Emotions I'd never felt before clutched my heart into a vise that was nearly debilitating in its pain. I clenched my hands into fists by my sides in direct violation of their deepest desire.

He destroyed all my good intentions when we walked out the door and his hand found my clenched fist and molded itself perfectly to me. We both immediately relaxed. He looked down at our hands in shock.

"Forgive me. I am unsure what has come over me. I did not mean to take liberties." He moved to let go of me and I held on tighter.

"Raif, please. It's harmless. I think we both feel better touching, even though I don't understand why. I need to feel better right now though, so please, just hold my hand." If he knew what it cost me to admit to needing another person's comfort, he never showed it. He was distracting me from my first glimpse of an island that before today I thought was only a myth told to give hope to those who lived in oppression.

This place brought out hushed tones; it was a place of refuge and respect. It was more pure than any cathedral I'd ever stepped foot in and more beautiful than any garden found on any magazine cover. It quite literally took my breath away with its splendor.

A stone path led away from Raif's house. The stones were a deep russet, and I'd never seen any like them before. They were multifaceted like a ruby, and led to a road of packed dirt. From there, I saw two more red stone paths meandering away, but couldn't see where they led, or much else past the solid dirt road as massive trees blocked most of my view. They towered higher than any skyscraper I'd seen at home; the tops lost in the cloud cover. There were big, white, fluffy clouds scattered throughout the blue sky, almost completely hiding the shimmer of something beyond.

"Wow." My exclamation was hushed, more of an exhalation of breath at the natural serenity. "It's even more beautiful than I could have dreamed about. Raif, how do you live in such beauty and not weep for its perfection? Is everything as amazing as you in this place?" I'd stopped to take everything in, blushing as I realized what I'd said and how I'd said it.

I tugged at his hand to continue walking, hoping he wouldn't notice the color in my cheeks. The red stone felt spongy, and I moved closer to the edge to inspect the flowers. In the middle of a massive forest that seemed to be immaculately tended, there were flowers and foliage taller than me. I was certain they had to be fake. The blooms were as big as my head and when I leaned in to smell them, the fragrance was intoxicating. The purity and beauty of the forest brought tears to my eyes.

Something moved in my peripheral and I clenched tighter to Raif's arm. A small herd of deer with large, moose-like antlers were starting to drive their young across our path into Raif's yard, where there were herds more each nibbling on the grass next to his home.

He lived in the middle of a naturally forming forest field. I'd seen them before when I'd taken Ashlyn hiking in the mountains. But none were as large as the space he occupied. I was following Raif, trailing slightly behind but still holding his hand. There were rabbits and all sorts of wildlife meandering through the field, unbothered by our presence. Butterflies of all colors flitted from flower to flower. They flew off in a cloud of rainbow wings to find another place to rest, changing the color and design of the flower completely without their multicolored wings to distract the eye.

The path we were on was hidden in shade from the trees, and it was very cool. I couldn't believe the colors and the wildlife that were milling about in this small area. Raif had to tug my hand a few times to get me moving away from my visual exploration of this small field and the forest beyond.

"You wanted our story, Natasha, but perhaps we should start with a geography lesson first?" He was smirking at me, his teal eyes dancing with barely restrained laughter.

I laughed, the sound echoing off the trees. The animals looked up, but none seemed concerned about my expression of joy. Raif laughed too, and it was like music to my soul. His bass chuckle blended perfectly with my higher pitched one.

"That'd be wonderful, Raif. This is unlike any place I've ever seen before. It's unlike anything I've even dreamed of. You have a beautiful home."

"Come, I will explain while we walk. You still must meet with the king and the priests. Atlantis was formed with the rest of the world, millennia ago. My descendants lived on the surface with you. Over eleven thousand years ago, there was a war, and we were thrust into the ocean. It is understandable that your people have reduced us to myth, when I am certain that many things of that time were thrust into legend. That is the story we will discuss later, now is just geography." I listened in amazement as we walked along, hand-in-hand. His words weren't quite able to distract me from the beauty surrounding us, rather they enhanced everything, his deep bass tones soothing and exciting me at the same.

"The world was created; each part was equally distributed to different gods. They did not quarrel amongst themselves at which section they received, instead they took their part and molded it into a land that they were pleased with. Poseidon was allotted with Atlantis. It was just a hunk of mountainous land when he started with it, the tallest of peaks being at the center of the island. It was at the base of this mountain that Poseidon created his temple and the main palace. It is the heart of Atlantis. He divided the rest of the land into rings with four floating sentries. The land of Atlantis is extremely fertile; anything that is planted and tended will grow here without difficulty thanks to Poseidon. He gathered all types of the differing animals that were ever created, and brought them to Atlantis to thrive. Poseidon loves variety, and created a land where all could live and thrive. He divided his central island, the only island actually called Atlantis, to be set apart from the rest. It is only accessible from a bridge that was created, with Poseidon's blessing, by his people.

"The second island rings the center and is called Melic. It holds the king's first uncle who is second in line to the throne. The island was originally divided in half for the different princes to rule, however this changed after we sank. It is only ruled by one now. There is a hearty bunch of both people and wildlife that thrive upon that island ring. It is a harsher land, though, as it is almost completely mountainous.

"Wait, how can it be both harsh and fertile? That seems impossible," I interrupted. The ground had shifted once we left the beautiful haven of his home, the red rock giving way to a pale path interspersed with the first normal thing I'd seen since I'd arrived—dull, gray stone.

"The land was divided by the brothers, however the land itself is not equally divided. We will walk through the only inhabited portion—the plain—on our way to the heart of Atlantis. Our people used to inhabit the rough mountains, but after we sank, we as a people changed." He paused as in reflection, or to remember where he was in his lesson, I couldn't tell. His expressive face held a mask of indifference I wasn't used to. Not that I'd had a particularly long time to become used to him, or that I ever would, but it struck me as a bit odd.

"The two rivers that surround Melic on either side of the ring help with the defense of the main island. There are two castles on Melic, one in the plains and one in the mountains. The mountains are a mixture of a steep, rocky terrain and a vast forest spreading like a blanket upon the hills. It is truly a dark beauty. There are three land bridges connecting Melic to Sumner, the third island and the one we are currently on, however two of the three bridges have not been in use for centuries."

He paused in his telling. The ground had shifted again, the stone becoming packed dirt that had clearly been walked on frequently. The dirt path jutted out toward another land mass. This was one of the bridges he was talking about. It wasn't a bridge in the sense I was used to, but an arched land mass that connected the two island rings together.

"How does this happen?" I asked.

"We built the bridge from two solid, interlocking pieces of orichalcum. We then covered it with soil and let nature resume her growth. Sumner is mostly a forested land. Interspersed throughout the forest are pockets of fields that some have used to create their housing, as you saw with mine. It was also originally divided for three princes, but it too diminished in its ruling after the war. Currently, Poseidon's second child's son, who is the third in line for the throne, rules Sumner. He tends to the forest and makes sure the herds that are to be provisionary to our survival, remain thriving. All types of creatures live on this island, as we are the easiest island to maintain. It is a mostly flat land that is easy to cultivate and farm. I think it is even better than that of the mainland, as it only has a few mountains." His voice held a note of pride that caused me to smile.

"The last ring is not really a ring of land, but four small islands set at the compass points. The northern one is called Rotsem and it is a tropical forested land with little fields that contain a variety of life. The eastern island faces the dry mountainous area of Melic and is called Horindu. It is a very dry, volcanic land that does not thrive with water. The southern island houses fields of flowers; it hosts the last remainder of our fertile plain and is called Diampri. The final island is in the west and is called Azazeil. It is a forested land with a natural occurring fountain of spring water in the center. Only on the main island of Atlantis does this fountain occur again."

How Raif thought I'd be able to focus on anything besides him was beyond me. We walked over the bridge just as he was speaking about it. What he didn't say was that it was the width of two semis stretched end to end, and nearly three times that in length. We didn't cross paths with anyone, but did make room on occasion for a pack of elephants to pass. Not once did I see signs of transportation other than by foot, nor did I really see a need; however, I'd been anticipating flying cars zipping by using banana peels for fuel. I'd always heard stories of how technologically advanced Atlanteans were. I was also very humbled to be able to walk in a land that had been under miles of ocean for thousands of years.

Before too long, we had made our way across the island of Melic, and were finally on the mainland of Atlantis. The mountain in the center was huge. It started almost as soon as we crossed the bridge and went up. The peak was hidden beyond the clouds that circled. The climb was surprisingly casual as we walked toward the temple and palace beyond. They were both nestled closer to the base of the mountain, but high enough that they overlooked the land below. The buildings were made of marble, silver, gold, and that same reddish material of the path.

"Raif, what is that red stone, and why is it only in a few spots? It's beautiful." I pointed to the path that we were on, as well as the two buildings that we could see in the distance.

"It is called orichalcum. It is a rare metal only found in abundance here. It is meant to designate the royal houses. The only roads it can be used on lead to the princes' homes, or in this case, to the king's castle and Poseidon's temple. It is only to be used in the building of any further temples to Poseidon, or the king's living quarters. Even the princes are forbidden to use it in their homes. It is nice looking, however I am partial to the opal. I love its softness, and the colors that can be found if it is cut properly."

"Wait a second. That orichalcum was in the path that led to your house." I stopped in my tracks.

"Yes. I am the third in line. The king's future son will hopefully replace him. If he does not produce an heir, my uncle will take the throne. There are two ahead of me before I even risk that torture. I tend to my lands, and make sure my people are cared for. I have no desire to be king." He spoke casually as he continued on. I hurried to catch up and hold his hand.

"You're a prince…a freaking royal. I'd never have guessed that you'd be royalty. You're so kind and generous I just thought you were a normal person. Well, not normal, wonderful, amazing and freaking perfect are better descriptors than normal, but you understand what I mean, right?" Thankfully we had just arrived at the palace, and I took advantage of our surroundings to distract him from my babbling admiration. "How can we see the sunset this far underwater?" I asked as I caught sight of the brilliant colors.

"It is one of the mysteries of Poseidon. There are still seasons. The sun, the moon, and weather patterns occur as naturally here as they do on the surface. Time is sometimes skewed from your world to ours, according to Poseidon's mood, but our days still match the length of yours. The protective dome that encircles us is the biggest mystery. We must have complete faith and trust in Poseidon that it remains intact to protect us from sudden and instant death. We also do not fully understand how Surface Dwellers arrive here. I will explain the things we do know after out meeting with King Nereus." He drew my attention from the impossible sight of the setting sun to the simple, yet elegant castle in front of me. It was gently tucked into the mountain with a small moat surrounding it. A stout bridge led the way into the castle, and the road we were on meandered around and higher up the mountain.

I held Raif's hand like a lifeline as we walked into the building. On either side of the drawbridge, imbedded into the castle were two statues: one a striking man with a trident, the other a woman of such beauty she took my breath away.

"Raif, who's that?" I whispered. "I mean, that man is clearly Poseidon, but I've never heard of a woman associated with him." He chuckled; the base sounds reverberated and made my whole body shiver in carnal response.

"You are an inquisitive woman, Lady Natasha. It is a statue of Cleito, and if you would be patient, I would tell you the tale of how we came to be here, as well as our origins, to which Cleito plays in integral part. You will discover in due time that she is Poseidon's *amada*, and the reason we are here."

I had so many questions, but the look on his face told me I'd have to wait for him to reveal anything else of his history. I wanted to hear him speak of his home and history more than I wanted to meet the Council and the king, but it didn't appear I had much of a choice. I trusted Raif instinctively to protect me during this meeting, but I was still nervous. It was terrifying to realize that I could give this stranger my absolute trust without a second thought. All I wanted at this moment was to go home with him and listen as he talked. I also found it unsettling to realize that home to me was starting to become anywhere he was. Even with my unsettled nerves I was more at peace with him than I'd ever been in my entire life. Instinctively I knew that here, miles below the ocean, with a man I hardly knew, I would always be safe, protected, and loved beyond measure.

8

We walked into the throne room and were greeted by what felt like every Atlantean on the islands. They were packed into a very large auditorium facing a dais in the front of the room, where there sat a row of chairs. A hush fell upon the crowd as we walked in, and every head turned in our direction. The people were very normal looking, if luminescent skin covering muscular bodies, with hair and eyes colors only found in the sea could be called normal. For some reason I had been expecting them to look like bug-eyed aliens, or some other mutated creatures that had yet to be identified. The only difference between the Atlanteans and myself was the skin, hair, and eye color. Well, that, and the fact that no one here had an ounce of body fat on them. The women were all thin with compact figures and lean muscles defining what I could see of their bodies. I could tell that they were used to hard labor.

The men were all muscular. No one that I saw had the couch warrior look to him or her. It was a sea of eye candy. I'd never felt like more of an outsider as I looked at the astonished faces of the people looking at me. My plush curves were definitely out of place here. It took me a few uncomfortable seconds to fully realize that they weren't just staring at me, but at us. Raif was clinging to my hand so tightly I could feel him trembling. I looked into his face and saw a mask of indifference plastered there, such a departure from how his eyes had been lit before we'd entered the room. This was not the same man I was falling for. This man was cold, calculated.

"Raifuku, you have been honored by Poseidon this day. Please bring your human here so that we may begin with the celebrations." The tenor voice echoed through the hushed building. The people parted, leaving a direct route to the dais, where the seats were filled by those I could only assume were the Council and the king.

The man speaking was the king. Even without a crown, he held an air of importance that could not be ignored. He also looked strikingly like the statue I'd noticed outside. He had the same wide-set eyes and prominent Roman nose of the statue. His hair was ruffled in a much more modern fashion than the statue's long pulled back mane, but at a glance I could tell that he was a descendant of Poseidon's. Raif's hand tightened even further on mine, and I knew if he didn't lighten up, he'd break it. I gently squeezed his hand and started rubbing my thumb across it. If I weren't looking for a sign of him relaxing, I would have missed the imperceptible loosening of his hand on mine, and the slight exhalation of breath.

As we moved through the crowd, I could hear whispered murmurs behind me. Raif tensed, but I couldn't understand why. His expression gave nothing away.

Once we'd drawn up directly in front of the king, Raif crossed his arms and bowed. He had to let go of my hand to bow properly, and I immediately began to shake. I had no idea when or how it happened, but I had become dependent on him for comfort, and I didn't like that. It took me a few moments to compose myself while he was talking.

"My lord, may I present Poseidon's gift—Lady Natasha from the Surface. We beg forgiveness for our tardiness, but I felt it inappropriate to introduce such a wonderful blessing from Poseidon in a state unbefitting a lady." He said all this as he rose from his bow, but didn't make any move to hold my hand again when he was finished. I was shocked to hear him speak with absolutely no inflection in tone or facial expression. I was starting to wonder who the real Raif was and if I had even a snowflakes chance in Hell to get my heart back if this was his true self. I did my best to curtsy as he finished talking.

"She is not like Poseidon's other gifts, is she? I wonder what he had in mind by sending her. She does not seem fit to tend fields, climb mountains, or care for our sea creatures. There is an excess to her that does not seem proper for a lady. She is not even properly contained in her dress; the spillage is extensive." At this, the king swatted the tops of my breasts as if to accent the 'excess' that he was talking about. I was beet red in anger and he wasn't even finished.

"She does possess motherly hips, perhaps she was sent here to breed. What say you, Raifuku? She would make an excellent breeder, and we are sorely lacking in new mothers." At this he grabbed my hips, pantomiming exactly what the process of breeding would entail, from behind me. I was enraged and extremely embarrassed to be treated like a piece of cattle, especially in front of so many people. I schooled myself slightly to hide the shame, but let my anger loose.

"I don't give a flying rat's ass what *Raifuku* has to say about it." I emphasized the use of his full name. "*She* has a name, and a mind of her own to choose whether she wants to be a breeder. She can talk for herself, you pompous ass! Who the hell are you to criticize me? I'm a strong woman who has a hell of a lot more to offer than ovaries. If you cared to ask me what I wanted instead of treating me like cattle, you'd know that I don't even want to be here. I just want to go home!" I spoke quickly, yanking myself out of his embrace and was visibly shaking with anger.

It took every ounce of restraint I had not to beat the crap out of this man, royalty or not. Raif had, at some point, put a restraining hand on my back, and even the warmth of his electric touch hadn't been able to calm me down. I knew I wasn't a wisp of a woman; that I had curves and cushion where there could be ribs and a six-pack, but I liked my appearance. Who was he to insinuate that I was unacceptable? Any softening toward this place I was starting to feel because of Raif vanished at this introduction. I desperately wanted to go home and pretend I had never seen Atlantis. The thought of never seeing Raif again was the only pain I felt. While that thought hurt beyond measure, I could never live in a place where I was so thoroughly disrespected because of my packaging.

"Well, she certainly has spirit. Atreyu, what has Poseidon whispered in your ear about this new treasure?" He laughed at me and turned away like I mattered less than a gnat buzzing around his head. If Raif didn't have one of my hands in his and his other on my back in a comfortable distraction, I swear I'd have hit the king of Atlantis right then and there. No wonder the queen's chair was still empty.

The man he turned to wore black robes that contrasted with his silver hair. His long locks were held back with a black cord. He had three long silver braids on the left side of his face that were separated out from the rest. He glided over to the king and started examining me like I was a piece of meat to be auctioned off later. His silver eyes swirled as he looked at me and for just an instant I saw an expression of awe, respect, and abject terror. He turned from me and addressed the king.

"My lord, as Poseidon's high priest I am honored to have had him visit his temple this day. He came to me and instructed me to find the ancient scrolls. He spoke to me again and told me that this day could be a day of much rejoicing or great despair. My king, Poseidon brings to all of Atlantis on this day, the one who will fulfill the prophecy." He gestured to me as a sudden uproar exploded from the crowd, distracting me from my questions and fury.

There were exclamations of joy, shock, and terror. I couldn't understand anything they said, but I could feel the undercurrents of emotions and see the expressions on their faces. The Council members continued to wear masks of indifference. Even Raif's face held no sense that he was concerned in any way that I was some sort of prophecy come true. Only the hand that clenched mine betrayed his emotions. Every muscle was tight with the tension he was holding in check. The king quickly hid his terror from his people, but not so quickly that I didn't catch the momentary lapse in his schooled features.

"Atreyu, are you certain this creature is whom Poseidon refers to? I cannot see how she would be anyone's *alma xemelga*." The king turned up his nose at me. I suppressed a shiver of awareness at the words. *Alma xemelga.* The words rang as important and resonated true feelings in me, although I didn't understand what they meant.

"King Nereus, I have not been Poseidon's high priest for eleven thousand years by misinterpreting his words, especially when he states them directly to me in his temple. He has not visited his temple since we sank. That alone marks the beginning of the prophecy. She is the key." He was angry with the king for questioning him. The walls of the palace started to shake, and I gripped Raif's arm, fearful. I hated earthquakes and this didn't make any sense. No one else seemed to be concerned, and the trembling only lasted seconds.

"What are we to do then?" King Nereus sighed as he gracefully fell into his seat and looked expectantly at Atreyu. I had thought it was a rhetorical question, but apparently, he needed answers.

"Poseidon also reminds me that, like us, she does have free will. She does not have to fulfill the prophecy at any stated date, if ever. There is also the possibility that if she is quarantined she will never meet her *alma xemelga.* She has only had physical contact with our immovable Raifuku and his apprentice, Michael. As is apparent by his lack of emotion, she was unable to break through Raifuku's defenses, and since Michael is tending to temple duties and not pining for her, we can be assured that she has not found her *alma xemelga* quite yet. You forget that I was around when Poseidon and Cleito walked these shores together and I am intimately aware of the effects of finding one's *alma xemelga.*" He paused for a moment. "We do have another option. We need not ever fulfill the prophecy if we destroy this Surface Dweller. Be warned, though, those that went against Poseidon in the past suffered greatly for it. I know the pull of one's *alma xemelga is* great, and Poseidon has yearned for the day when he can reunite with Cleito again."There was an instant hush at his words. Some shed tears at the mention of Poseidon and Cleito; others looked around in fear at the mention of her name.

"My king, if I may." Raif's bored tone echoed around the room. "Perhaps we should take some time to discuss the options further. It might be a good idea to open the door to our fellow Atlanteans to bring their desires and concerns to you as this affects us all. Atreyu can continue to consult the scrolls and discuss the matter further with Poseidon. Perhaps there is another way the prophecy can be fulfilled at a later date. Or, when Lady Natasha is fully briefed, she can be part of the decision. Must anything be decided now? This is a time of celebration; Poseidon has gifted us with a female after years of silence. I will take her to my home with me so that she remains under constant guard and will have no further contact with any Atlanteans, thereby eliminating the opportunity for her to create a bond. We shall return the instant the decision is made to hear your ruling. Is this sufficient for the Council?" Silence fell over the room after Raif's speech.

"Hey—" I was cut off by a painful grip on both my hand and hip as Raif swept me behind him. Apparently Raif sensed that I was going to ask to just be sent home. I held my tongue. I trusted Raif enough to get me out of here without them opting to kill me.

"Raifuku speaks with the sort of knowledge and foresight that should have been delivered to King Atlas before we joined the last war. We will open court tomorrow for all who wish to voice their concerns either for or against the destruction of this woman. She will remain Raifuku's prisoner and all are forbidden to associate with her. When the sun rests in three days, the Council shall convene again to either fulfill the prophecy or eliminate the cause for concern. It is so decreed. May Poseidon bless you with clear skies and strong winds at your back." With Nereus' words, Raif took hold of me. He turned me to face him.

"Natasha, I apologize for this, but I need you to close your eyes and allow me to carry you. I will explain everything when we get home," he whispered, so softly I barely heard him. Though his whispered words carried concern, his face, which was visible to every Atlantean in the crowd, only showed boredom.

He quickly scooped me up and threw me over his shoulder in a fireman's carry so I could stare at his backside. My protests died as soon as they started. He had a very nice butt. I held on tight, but there was no way I was closing my eyes from this view. He turned and hurried out of the building with determined strides.

I couldn't help but picture his face with a firm expression on it, daring anyone to approach him. I watched as feet turned away from us, until they completely disappeared from my viewpoint. We cleared the building and Raif swept me from his shoulder to his arms, holding me like I was cherished. He ran to his home. We were there within minutes with his stride and speed. He was barely out of breath.

"Okay, Raif, you can put me down now and tell me what is going on." He set me down in his living room and started pacing. I didn't know whether I should go to him, or let him come to me. In my mind those were the only two options. I was also trying to maintain my indignant anger at how I'd been treated. My blood boiled just thinking about the hundreds of strangers convening to decide my fate as if I were an inconvenience. "Raif, please talk to me. I have to know what's going on."

I tried to intercept him during one of his passes, but he evaded me. As he passed I could hear him mumbling in another language. Suddenly he stopped and let out an inhuman roar. It reminded me of the lions I'd seen on television, claiming their prey. I backed away slowly, not knowing which Raif to expect from moment to moment, fearful for the first time in his presence.

"Raif. Please calm down, or tell me what I can do to help you. Please, I need you right now. What the hell just happened? Why is my life hanging in the balance?" Tears slid down my face and for once I didn't care. I was terrified. In no way was I ready to die. I wanted to choose life, even if it meant staying prisoner here. I would miss my family terribly, but I would live with that sorrow if it meant I could live.

"Poseidon! Why her? Why bring her to me if you are just going to take her away? How have I offended you to be punished in this manner? Why must I endure this suffering and pain? Answer me, Poseidon! I know you are there." He fell to the ground, his shoulders shaking. His hair hid his face from me, but the words that left him were angry, bitter, and tight with suppressed tears. "Oh, what a cruel game the fates play. Natasha, I cannot even wish that you had never been brought here, for I cherish every second I have had in your presence. I don't know why we were chosen to start setting the wheels of change in motion. I wondered at the feelings and had hoped to inquire of Atreyu the extent of them as well as continue to explore them with you. I have never felt this way about another living being in my eleven thousand years of life, and now know I never will again. Three marvelous days is all I will have to hold onto in my memories when we could have had an eternity of happiness together. This is a true injustice being placed on us." His voice cracked and shook. He wouldn't make eye contact with me.

"Raif, please, just tell me what's going on." My heart was breaking at the sight of him hunched on the carpet, shoulders shaking and alone. I started inching closer to comfort him but remained wary of his ever-changing emotions.

"We are left with only one option, as I am not capable of allowing them to destroy you. I must take you to Cleito and hope she has devised a way to transport you back to the surface. Offering a false option to the people has satisfied them for now, but I will not allow them the choice to take your life. Having an *alma xemelga* is truly the most wonderful and terrible thing in the world." He started mumbling to himself and I desperately tried to follow his one-sided conversation. "There is still a small chance that they will let you live. We could keep our feelings secret and you could remain my willing prisoner for the rest of eternity. Perhaps they will see reason in this matter where they had not before." He looked up at me with such hope and terror mixed in his expression that my heart broke all the remaining restraint I had. I smoothed back his black hair and wiped the tear-streaks from his cheeks with trembling fingers.

"There was fear in Nereus' eyes. No. He will not let you live." He bowed his head. "Even if everyone else votes to keep you, I don't think he will honor their wishes." He whispered and I placed my hand on top of his head and ran my fingers down his silky tresses. Gently, I lifted his face to mine. His anguished expression tore at every part of my heart. My soul wept with his. "Natasha." My name was a plea, filled with love and agony.

I lowered my head to his and kissed him. It was only meant to be a chaste kiss to ease his worried heart, but as he clutched my body to his, it grew. I slid to my knees to give him better access to my mouth. His hands slid up my back until they were fisted in my hair. He tipped my head back to hungrily feast at my mouth. Everything ceased to exist. We were the only two people in a world of nothingness. He was strong, demanding, needy, and yet so gentle.

I opened my mouth, accepting everything he had to offer. There wasn't a better place in the universe than in his arms. My hands explored every part of his neck and torso, memorizing every ripple, ridge, and dimple. Distantly, I heard myself whimper. He responded with an answering growl that vibrated his entire body. I shivered with excitement.

He pulled back and hesitated for a moment, but before he could say anything I started undoing his shirt. His words dried in his throat before they could even be uttered. Apparently I wasn't moving quickly enough for him, because he yanked the hated clothing from his body in one swoop. When his face appeared again, no longer hidden by his shirt, his expression was one of someone committing a sin. He schooled his features and looked at the ground.

"Forgive me! I was not—" I put my trembling fingers on his lips, halting his apology.

"Please. I need you." I kissed him again. This time I didn't even try to keep it chaste. I kissed him as if he was water and I was trapped in the desert. He removed my dress and we were finally skin to skin. I'd craved this moment from the first time I opened my eyes and saw him staring back at me. I shuddered in his arms, feeling the electric currents running through every pore of my body, into his, and back again. He lifted me into his arms and without breaking our kiss for even a moment he carried me, naked, to his bed. He placed me gently on the sheets and stepped back to stare at me longingly for a moment. I felt my necklace slide around to my back leaving a thin silver line around my neck as my only covering. He moved toward the bed and I held out a hand.

"Wait." I was breathless in my need for him.

"I did not mean to presume that we would be intimate. Forgive me." He bowed his head and moved to leave.

"No. I only wanted you to wait so you would take your pants off. No need to get off the bed twice. Remove them and come here." I held onto one arm so that he wouldn't disappear on me.

He smiled as if I'd just answered all his prayers and removed his pants. He stood there for an eternity just staring at me lying on his bed like a feast. My mouth dropped open as I gazed at his perfect body. I started to shiver slightly in fear as well as anticipation as he was huge. There was no way we were doing this without it hurting a little.

I pulled him to me and took his mouth with mine again. His hands explored my body, gently sliding up my arm and down my side. He stopped at the underside of my breast and smiled when I whimpered. He took my breasts in his large hands and swept his thumbs across my nipples. I was putty. He released my mouth to nurse at one breast and I came right then.

His right hand continued to play on the one breast as he licked and suckled the other. His left went exploring for my moist, heated center. He found the nub and I came again. No man had ever been able to play my body so well. I writhed and moaned on his bed, helplessly crying out for more. I needed him at that moment, more than I needed to take my next breath. I tried to reach down between us to touch him, but he moved. He placed his finger inside me and felt the effect he had on me.

He moaned and thrust his finger faster, adding a second. I was close again, begging him to join me. I desperately wanted to hold him if he wasn't going to enter me, just so he could feel the same release I was going to feel in a moment. My helpless whimpers caused him to smile with my nipple still sheathed in his mouth. He bit down as he continued to thrust with his fingers.

I could feel his member against my thigh as I met every thrust of his hand. Just as I started my climax, he pulled his fingers out and sheathed himself into me. I barely registered his size entering me as I screamed in ecstasy. He stayed still, letting me come down and breathe for a second before he started moving. My body was still reeling from the aftershocks and every slow thrust brought another small wave of excitement through me.

He looked intensely into my brown eyes with his teal ones and I knew he wasn't going to last long. He was so large that he rubbed every spot I didn't know I had. His slow thrusts were taking me higher than I'd ever thought possible. He kissed me and that seemed to be the conclusion to our joining. I exploded from the inside out. I felt every part of my body release to the universe in sheer bliss.

I saw images of my lonely life of responsibility intermingled with his. We shared more than the intimacy of making love. Our souls left our bodies to join each other and return as a fractured whole. They soared in ecstasy, in the knowledge that we'd finally come together. When my soul soared back into my body, I realized that Raif had passed out on top of me. The last thought I had before I blacked out was that he was a very heavy man.

9

Natasha? Love, are you all right?” Raif asked, his deep voice thick with concern and contentment.

I felt him snuggled behind me, rubbing a hand slowly up and down my arm. I was cradled protectively in his arms, facing the wall. I felt sore, and more at peace than I had any right to be. I was home for the first time in my life, and while I knew that thought should’ve terrified me, I was comforted by it. I turned in his embrace and looked at him. His face held an expression of peace that I subconsciously knew no one else had ever seen. I knew this was the man that held my heart. The man he’d been in front of the Council had been a façade to protect himself from the betrayal and politics of his life. I treasured being able to know the real Raif that he kept hidden from the rest of the world.

“That was amazing. If it’s always like that we’re likely to solve the problem of my destruction without the king’s interference. I’ve never felt this content before.” I smiled and kissed him slowly.

We enjoyed lazily exploring each other's mouths. Our hands slowly traced paths down backs and up arms. It was a simple enjoyment of touch more intimate than anything else I'd ever experienced. I knew deep into the recesses of my being that I loved this man with my entire heart. I pulled away and looked at him. He'd felt my necklace on my back and pulled it forward. At its sight, he stiffened in my arms.

"Where did you get this?" His voice trembled.

"I was sitting on the beach looking out at the ocean when I realized I was holding it. I'd thought I was sifting through shells at the time. I just thought it was beautiful and unique." My tone was a little defensive. For the first time since finding the stone, I felt uncomfortable wearing it. I started to take it off and he stilled my hands.

"Natasha, with what we have just shared I am going to demand that you do not play me for a fool. You did not get this on the surface. You got this from here. I know, because I made this after we sank and it has been missing. I had meant to place it on a chain for my future bride, but it was no longer in my box when I made the proper chain for it. I will ask you again, where did you find this?" His touch was no longer gentle and caring, but cold. I yanked the necklace off my neck and threw it at him as I jumped out of his bed.

"I am telling you the truth, asshole! I found the stupid thing on the shores of the Bimini Island and was captivated by it. I felt like it was a gift from the sea and I couldn't bring myself to get rid of it. Even showing other people caused me to feel possessive over it. I bought this chain for it on the same island and haven't been able to part with it since. I had no idea it was from here or that you'd made it. Since it's that important to you, take the stupid thing back. I certainly don't want to hold something that's so obviously meant for someone else." When I'd finished, I stormed into his bathroom to bathe so that he wouldn't see me cry. I felt foolish, like an unruly child. Everything was so intense here, things happened so quickly and I hadn't had time to think about anything. I had watched his face as I yelled at him and knew the moment he realized I was telling the truth, the emotions crossing his face confused and scared me. I didn't hear him come in, with the water spraying my face, but felt his arms pull me close to his body.

"Forgive me, *amada*. I should have known that Poseidon sent it for you. He somehow knew you were meant for me and wanted to give us his blessing. I was just shocked to have seen it again. He must have known you were mine and claimed you as such before we met. It is yours; it always has been and always will be. You are my *alma xemelga* and I am yours. Please don't cry. I was wrong to be angry with you." He stroked my back in circles and lifted my chin so I could see his face. "I cannot bear to see you upset, *amada*. Forgive me?" He kissed me. I was having difficulty dealing with emotions that had been sealed away behind a wall for most of my life, and wasn't comfortable with the vulnerability I felt around him. But I could no more hold a grudge against him than I could have held my bare hand in a flame.

After we'd showered, we dressed and laughed when both of our stomachs began growling. His kitchen was done in black marble and a darkly stained wood. I thought at this point the beauty of this place would have become normal, but I was wrong. There were herbs drying above the center counter as well as in the open pantry. I was surprised to see modern, if not higher-tech appliances in the kitchen of a man who seemed so comfortable with the archaic. Everything was gorgeous and would make the most seasoned chefs jealous.

I sat on a barstool and watched him move around the kitchen. I craved him on a base level that was disturbing in its intensity. Without doing anything, he was tempting.

"To understand the predicament we are in now, you must understand our history. You remember me telling you that when we were created the gods had divided the earth and created their lands to suit their needs?" He looked up with his piercing teal eyes and waited for affirmation.

It was luck that a nod was acceptable, as that was all I was capable of at that moment. All rational thought left me at the sight of his face framed by the inky black of his loose, wet hair. I attempted to hide my reaction from him, but the corners of his mouth still curved in a knowing grin.

"Well, there existed a time before that and a time even before that, which has been lost in its telling. The time before the division of lands was when the three brothers ruled the planet. Zeus commanded all living things, Poseidon, the land and the waters, and Hades was tricked by his brothers into ruling the underworld. Zeus shared the power of the humans' love with his brothers and the lesser gods. As long as tribute was made to the three brothers, the lands prospered. The people worshiped Zeus and Poseidon, and they in turn rewarded the people with fertile lands and their protection. It was a relatively peaceful time and the gods, excluding Hades, were content to let things be."

"Everyone's heard this story. It's a myth. The gods battled, Hades lost, they all disappeared," I interrupted, hoping to lead him past a pseudo history lesson. He looked at me, withering any further desire for interruption.

"Hades had always prided himself on his cunning intellect and was incensed that Zeus and Poseidon had been able to trick him into ruling the underworld. He was the only god that did not benefit from the praise and the love of the people. He was forced to live on the torment of the deceased's misery.

"Zeus and Poseidon thought to contain Hades retribution by depleting his power source, as it is almost impossible to gain strength from the dead. In his fury, Hades conspired with the fates, who have always loved a good deception, and had the souls of every living being divided."

"Wait. What do you mean that Hades lived on torment? I thought gods could only gain power if they received praise. That's why Hades stole Hera's daughter, so he would have one living soul to shower him in adoration, right?"

"Not really, that is more a twist humans have placed on this tale to make Hades more a tyrant than he really is. You see, as Zeus and Poseidon gained power with the love and worship of their people, Hades' power had transformed and started to grow with the tortured pain of every soul that had departed from the living world. What better way for him to gain in power than by splitting the souls, ensuring that not only would he have twice the amount of suffering, but they would suffer all the more by being incomplete? He also knew that by being incomplete, the people would turn away from the gods in their search for their *alma xemelga* thus depleting the power base of his enemies."

"That's a terrible thing to do. Hades is kind of a dick. What does *alma xemelga* mean?"

Raif's mouth split into a grin. "Yes, well, I guess he could be defined in such terms, but then so could the other gods. *Alma xemelga* means 'soul mate' or 'my other half' in Atlantean. May I continue?" I nodded, smiling to myself as he started putting bacon and eggs on plates. It was such a normal thing; I almost forgot we were talking about ancient Greek mythology as if it were actual fact. "The arrangement with the fates created chaos. The fates thrived on chaos, relishing in every moment that they could make the gods' lives miserable." He looked up at me, his teal eyes piercing into mine with a flare of anger I didn't expect. It did weird things to my insides, none of which belonged to fear. "Life has always been nothing more than a game to the fates. They have never been alive nor dead, they have just always been. However, they did create stipulations to maintain some semblance of fairness. While they enjoyed chaos, they were careful to maintain a balance in power. It has never been said that the fates favored a certain god. The stipulations to this arrangement were that each soul would only spend a hundred years in Tartarus, the place your people call Hell, at which time they were allowed to be reborn to search for their mate again. There is no limit on how many times a soul can be reborn, just that, until it finds its mate, it is to suffer. Once a soul found its mate, they would pass over the underworld to enter into the Summerland to live in peace. This was agreeable to Hades, as he knew the souls would suffer that much more each time they returned to him.

"Hades was tricked this time by his own arrangement, for he is also a living being, as are all the other gods. By his own specifications, all living souls were to divide, leaving both man and god in search for their other half. As Hades has no contact with any living being, he will never be able to combine his soul. You can only merge with your mate if you both still live."

"So, what about Persephone? I know you said that was a twist, but what does that mean? Hades has no chance to find his mate? That seems rather unfair, even if he was being a jerk to start all this."

"Persephone is Hades' wife. They were married prior to the soul split. For thousands of years she split her time between the living and the dead, but she has since found her mate and no longer travels to the underworld. Hades remains alone. I am uncertain if he has any way of recognizing his mate, or if that was the cost of the curse he chose to place upon his brothers and the world."

We ate in silence for a moment. I thought about what Hades had done, if his punishment was justified. To never have the opportunity to find your other half? It was unimaginable pain. But to have been the cause—I wasn't sure if that was fair or not. It wasn't my place to decide, and for that I was grateful. Raif started again in a softer tone.

"It is said that once the soul has mated, it shares the body of the two until the physical beings depart from this world. Usually the deaths occur very close together or simultaneously as the bodies have become attached at a deeper level than if the soul had not merged.

The soul needs constant physical affirmation of acceptance to maintain its connection. Although, if that is true than Cleito has truly gone mad." He trailed off for a moment and we ate in silence.

"Who's Cleito?" I finally asked. I felt troubled, but not for myself. It was as if I was feeling a muted version of the turmoil going on inside Raif. Which was weird and I dismissed it as some funky thing that happens in Atlantis.

"When the *dividir alma* occurred, gods and mortals felt it. There was an instantaneous rumble across the entire earth that echoed into the heavens. I am told that the split sent many into madness. You can surely understand how a person would feel at having part of his essence ripped from him." He shuddered. "Zeus decided it would be better for the gods to find their mates if the lands were split, and created into images of what that particular god desired. People, he had discovered over the years, were generally born into a land where they would thrive. He deduced that in order to become whole again, he would have to rule and live in a place where his soul would be reborn, a place where *he* thrived. He divided the lands so each god could search for their mates, for having incomplete gods was not acceptable.

"When Poseidon was allotted this particular piece of land, he was pleased. It was still young in its formation, so he was able to bend every part to his will. He walked around his land to understand the people, acquainting himself with what the land could offer them so that he would get the maximum amount of praise.

"Even though the gods now searched for their *alma xemelga* as one with us, they still needed our love and acceptance to gain power. They are to strive for our happiness, just as we are to theirs, to maintain utopia. Part of the happiness on both sides is to find our *alma xemelga*. Poseidon was pleased with his territory for a number of reasons. The first reason was that water surrounded this land; it is his element of choice. The most unforeseen, was the discovery of his *alma xemelga*." Raif nodded to me, indicating that he was finally about to answer my question. "Cleito was the daughter of a farmer and very beautiful. She was devoted to her family and her father adored her. He was not particularly fond of the gods and had been hoping that their small island would be overlooked as too insignificant for any of the gods to want. When he saw Poseidon walking toward his farm that fateful day, he was less than pleased.

"There was no mistaking the instant connection between Cleito and Poseidon. The moment their eyes met, life for them, and us as a people, instantly changed. The soul recognized its mate, wanting to meld even before the two bodies had a chance to be introduced. It was said that the earth shook with their meeting, lightning cracked, and the waters churned in delight. I'm told that there has never been anything like it. I was not there for their meld and have never witnessed another *alma se funden*."

"What does that mean? *Divider alma* must have something to do with the curse, right? What does the other one mean?" I was enthralled.

"*Divider alma* is the Atlantean term for 'soul split,' its literal translation is 'divided soul.' *Alma se funden* is the wondrous time when the soul meets its other half and becomes complete again, sharing the twin bodies. It is supposed to be glorious. It literally means 'soul meld.'" He smiled at me and I shivered. "Poseidon knew before the day was over that Cleito was to be protected and cherished at all costs. He continued to form this land with the sole purpose of protecting his mate from any harm. The other gods mocked him for the futility of loving a mortal woman and he chastised them for their lack of completion. Zeus married Cleito and Poseidon before the week's end and they lived together in the castle we visited yesterday. Poseidon was inclined to grant his bride anything she desired—we were lucky that she was not a selfish woman and just asked that their people be cared for. She desired only that the land would be forever fertile and their people never want for anything.

"Poseidon would watch her as she interacted with the people. His heart would burst with pride and joy that this woman, who was so giving of herself, was his mate. He was terrified of losing her. It was unknown as to what the effects the *dividir alma* had on the soul once it melded into one being with two bodies, especially when one of those bodies was an immortal god and the other was human.

"He placed wards on this land protecting her from any unforeseen harm and ensuring that only age would be her end. When he was assured of this precaution he also created natural occurring spring fountains that extended vitality. There are three that exist here." I held my hand up, not knowing if I could believe what I was hearing.

"You mean to tell me that you have the Fountain of Youth here?" My disbelief was evident.

"We have three."

"Like, the Fountain of Youth that the conquistadors searched for, killed for, and never found because it's not real?"

"Similar to how no one has found Atlantis in over eleven thousand years, no? The entire continent of people has faded into myth. Your people allow history to fade and change until you no longer know truth from fiction. You accept truth only from those storytellers called historians, teachers, and doctors. Anyone who has an experience that varies from what they preach—you call them crazy. Your society has baffled me for centuries, yet you continue to thrive and grow; even through losing the connection to the lands, the energy, and the spirit around that makes the world such an amazing place."

I felt an anger that wasn't mine. I wasn't angry at his words, I was chastised by them. He was right. We do only believe those who have prestigious titles in their fields. If a professor of astronomy told us we were the only habitable planet in the entire universe, we would believe them over the person who said aliens exist. And here I was, talking to someone who was essentially an alien on an island that shouldn't be real, miles below the ocean floor. Who was I to say things couldn't be?

"How can you not believe in the magic of the fountains when you're here?" Raif's voice was pained.

"This is a lot to take in, Raif," I began. "I'm trying. Really, I am. It's difficult to wrap my mind around everything, but being here, seeing and touching things that shouldn't exist—well, it makes it difficult not to believe." His lips curved into the slightest of smiles and my heart stuttered. It was in that moment that I knew I would do anything to see joy on his face.

"When Cleito and Poseidon had their first set of twins," he continued, "Poseidon was so overjoyed, he named everything after his first son, Atlas. That was when we truly became a people with an identity separate from the rest of the world. From that moment on, we were known as Atlantis. He named the sea where we lived the Atlantic Ocean, and it was larger than any known body of water. I must admit, he was not very creative in naming things, but perhaps joy diminishes your mental capacity to a certain extent. They went on to have four more sets of twins and Atlantis was divided amongst them all. For a time, there were nine princes, one king, and Poseidon, god of it all.

"When Atlas came of age to rule, Poseidon took Cleito to their summer home on the cliffs. They lived in secluded bliss for a century, knowing their family would want for nothing. It was a mistake to have given complete control to mortal men, one we have paid for in blood and tears for eleven thousand years." His voice was sad with the destruction of their proud history.

"We have a metal that is only found here in abundance, and in extremely small pockets that are difficult to get to in other parts of the world. You asked me about it earlier; the red, multifaceted stone. We call it orichalcum. It is an amazing metal that can be used in just about everything. It is strong, yet can be melted to be handled as easily as fabric. Our fathers traded this metal for the chance to find our mates. As you can imagine we craved this more than anything else, and for all that we had, our lands were, and are still, mostly comprised of men. Trading the metal to other regions enabled us to have their females visit for a chance to find our *alma xemelga*.

"Few women who visited these famed islands could stand the isolation from the fast-paced cultures that other gods led. They would stay, search for their mate, then leave as quickly as possible. We lacked the variety of other lands, yet have never felt incomplete because of it. We had never been a people to force others to live on our lands against their natures, but we did trade fairly and pray to the gods that we would find our mates.

"King Atlas had begun to feel pressured to find a wife to produce further heirs, as we were, and still are, unsure of our lifespan. We do not live as you do, Lady Natasha. There is something about either living in Poseidon's lands or having his blood in our veins that makes us practically immortal. We also discovered that we have a very difficult time reproducing.

"Atlas had the same hopes as we all do, to find his mate and become complete. After sixty unsuccessful years of searching, he gave up and married one of Aphrodite's daughters, Triana."

"Aphrodite... Wasn't she the goddess of love, or something?"

"Yes, love and beauty. All her children shared her beauty, and Triana was no exception. Because of this, she was accustomed to being spoiled and pampered by her father and mother. Atlas felt burdened to spoil her in the way that she had been accustomed to because she had agreed to give up the chance of finding her mate to be with him. She was constantly draped in fine jewels and expensive, rare fabrics. She had the latest fashions sent to her for her approval upon their creation. Exotic perfumes were found or created just for her. Atlas doted on her, eventually becoming so enamored with her that our trade agreements changed to suit her needs and we no longer had time to search for our mates. We were too busy keeping our king and queen sated. Our treasury grew to be the most valued and coveted in the world. With news of our treasury and the vanity of Queen Triana, we quickly became prime targets for invasion and had many enemies.

"Atlas was a good leader in that he saw the threats and prepared for them. A better ruler would have avoided what was to come, petitioning to his god and father, Poseidon, for guidance and direction. Atlas, however, created a vast army and built walls around the borders of our lands, making it nearly impenetrable to attack. Our warriors were brutal in their defense of our lands so that not one single member of invading armies lived to tell the tales. Atlas was amazed at the brutality his people were capable of and became insatiable. We quickly became a warrior nation to be feared by all we approached.

"Atlas was cunning in his strategies for conquering other lands, and eventually he began to draw the attention of the gods. They watched with growing anger as our king desiccated their lands and Poseidon did nothing to contain him. For years we plundered and lived as gods among men. We were feared for our brutality, respected for our tenacity, and envied for our wealth. King Atlas declared himself the god of Atlantis." Raif paused and shrugged his shoulders, as if to erase the burden of his people's history.

"Triana gave Atlas a son the year we were destroyed. The day Prince Nereus was born was a fantastic day of celebration for all. Had we been attacked that day, we would have been defeated. For a week we drank to celebrate the health of Prince Nereus and the prowess of King Atlas. It was a joyous time of celebration that the gods used to destroy us.

"A scout arrived home a week after Prince Nereus was born, bringing news of an uncharted land filled with treasure that made ours look like a drop of water in the vast ocean. Queen Triana was incensed by this news and King Atlas immediately sent out our strongest warriors to obtain this treasure for his beloved wife. He depleted our army so that only a handful remained behind to defend our borders.

"We were attacked from all sides by three different armies. If we had all of our warriors we may have stopped the bloodshed of our people, but we will never know. I was just a boy when I saw them come. My father was the Warrior Chief and was among those sent out to the sea to obtain the treasure when we were attacked. I took up a sword and killed many before I was captured and brought to the castle with the rest of the young captives.

"Poseidon heard the cries of his people, but it was too late. Zeus was in our palace to enact the justice we deserved. Zeus told Poseidon of our treachery, explaining that if Poseidon was not going to lead his people, then he would suffer to watch as Zeus destroyed us. Poseidon allowed Zeus to kill his son, Atlas, and Triana, for their ambitious greed; as long as he was allowed to handle the insolence of his followers in a manner befitting our vanity. The invading armies were given one night to vacate our lands or they too, would suffer Poseidon's rage.

"The next day, with the rising sun, the grounds shook as a great earthquake started to swallow the lands. The seas boiled and raged sending tsunamis to flood the lands. Many people were killed, including some of Poseidon's own children, and we huddled in terror, knowing we were soon to follow.

"Cleito saved us from death. She cried out to her mate to have mercy on their people. She pleaded with him to have mercy on those that they had failed to protect, tears streaming down her face. Her tears melted Poseidon's heart of righteous anger and the shaking slowed. Poseidon agreed to spare the lives of their people, but was incensed that the tears of a woman had quelled him. He swore that they would never again be his downfall. Cleito bowed her head in supplication so he would not see the pain he was causing her.

"Poseidon planned to punish Cleito, but before he could, her body rose up and spoke a prophecy: 'A lesson must be learned for gods and men to live in harmony. Atlantis shall descend to be hidden. Until the time the soul mates and willingly chooses to break;

you shall be apart from your heart. Atlantis will join the ranks again when tears are freely given.' After speaking, Cleito fell to the ground. Poseidon became terrified that his anger had been the death of his mate and rushed to her side. As he touched her, the earth shook even more violently than before. For the first time ever, Poseidon was unable to bend the land to his will. He was abruptly cast out of Atlantis. We were swallowed by the seas; to be hidden from all until the prophecy could be fulfilled. Cleito wept for the loss of her mate, but no tears fell. Instead the heavens opened and it rained in Atlantis.

"We as a people imprisoned her in the palace where she had lived with Poseidon and she has remained captive and alone for the eleven thousand years that we have been underwater. She prays to the gods for forgiveness for her people, hoping for the day she will be reunited with Poseidon. He is allowed to enter his temple, but only when called and only as a shade. He has never entered though, choosing to abandon all communication with his people until the day he is to be reunited with his *alma xemelga*." Raif finished with a flourish.

"It's a sad story, Raif, but what does it have to do with us? Why is everyone so upset about my arrival? They don't think…I mean, we couldn't be…" I couldn't say the words I knew in my heart to be true. I couldn't be Raif's soul mate. We barely knew each other. But, if his story was to be believed, that didn't matter. Once your soul meets its match—that's it.

"You are most definitely my *alma xemelga*, my soul's mate. I had suspected it with my reaction to you when you woke here, but I was not certain until we shared a bed. You and I are to fulfill the prophecy that the oracle set into motion eleven thousand years ago. Without us, my people will be forced to live for eternity under water, never mating, never dying, forever living with the torment of knowing that the other half of their soul is lost without them." He reached for my hand and I grasped at his, looking for something to tether me down. I replied with as much honesty as I could through a voice that was soft and surprisingly steady.

"That really doesn't sound that bad, you know. So we mate. I'm not seeing the downfall here. Yeah, I'll miss my family, but for some reason I feel more at home with you than I've ever felt before. Why are you so upset? Would you rather have a different mate?" He chuckled at my naïveté and pulled me onto his lap.

"*Amada*, my beloved, we did not think it would take eleven thousand years for you to arrive. Many of my people have become content to live apart from those on the surface and are unwilling to be a part of a culture that is ruled by selfish people constantly at war. We are a peaceful people now." He took a breath and I could feel the faint tremors in his body. I held him close to me, resting my head on his shoulder to allow him to say what he needed to without having to look at me. "The second part of the prophecy is that we must willingly part. If we complete the *alma se funden* you must return to where you are from and leave me here. You must understand; time is of no consequence when you are dealing with immortal beings. You may leave and part from me for an unknown amount of time. It could be seconds, or millennia. I am not sure if I am capable of being apart from you for that long. There is a small chance that you could stay here, hidden with me, without mating. As long as my people do not know you are my *alma xemelga* we should be safe." He said regretfully, knowing his hope was foolish.

"Won't Poseidon be angry with us for prolonging his separation from Cleito? From everything you've said, it sounds like a bad idea to piss off your god."

"I know you are right, *amada*, but I don't like it. We will depart to Cleito's palace in the evening so that we can travel under the cover of darkness, away from my peoples' prying eyes. I believe she will be able to help us complete the prophecy and get you home."

10

Raif left to gather supplies. He told me to stay in the house and rest while I waited for him to return, we both needed to prepare for the long night ahead of us. We'd be at the base of the mountains to Cleito's prison by morning, and we'd be staying there until the next nightfall to avoid prying eyes. He had hope that she knew of a way to get me off this island. If not, he wasn't certain what we would do. But he held fast to his faith in Poseidon and their prophecy.

As strongly as he believed that I was his soul mate, the man didn't know me at all. There was no way I was going to stay cooped up in his house when there was a whole world to explore. I gave myself credit though; I stayed in the house for about an hour snooping through all his stuff. It wasn't as much fun as I thought it'd be, so I decided to go outside and take pictures. I didn't know if I'd be able to take my camera with me when I left, but I was hoping that I'd be returned with everything I arrived with.

I was in heaven. Atlantis was the most beautiful place I'd ever seen. The skies shimmered in perpetual sunset, with the colors reflecting on the dome protecting us. The clouds were pure white without the smog of a city to fade them. It was truly a shame to have to leave. I was happily taking pictures of the forest behind Raif's house when someone behind me spoke.

"You really are more attractive than the king gives you credit for, you know." I turned to see Michael leaning casually against a tree.

"Don't do that! You scared the crap out of me. What are you doing here, anyway? I was under the impression that Raif's house was forbidden to all you Atlantean people?" I attempted to hide the camera in the folds of my dress as I turned to face him.

"As I'm fairly certain you're already spoken for, I think I can bend the rules." Michael winked at me conspiratorially. "Besides, I'm not quite fully Atlantean and Raifuku sent me to make sure you didn't cause any mischief. It seems like I got here just in time. You do realize that there are people here who would kill you on sight, thereby eliminating the need for this pointless debate, right?" He smiled.

"What do you mean you're not fully Atlantean yet? What are you?" I sat down cross-legged in the grass so I didn't have to invite him inside alone with me. I made it a general rule to stay out in the open with men I didn't plan on sleeping with.

"I'm like you. I was born in Los Angeles in 1932. I was at a surfing competition during a hurricane in 1954 when the waves tossed me into a current and I drowned. I woke up outside the palace and have been Raifuku's loyal apprentice ever since. He teaches me things about Atlantis, and I teach him how to surf in the canals separating the islands. It isn't as much fun as the open ocean, but honestly, I've no idea what would happen to us if we attempted to surf beyond the shore. What year are you from?" He plopped down across from me. I grinned as I watched him chew on a piece of grass with his tanned, translucent blue skin.

"Can I take your picture? I don't even know if I'll be able to keep it, but I really want to try." I held up my camera and waited for his approval.

"Why not? I doubt you'll be able to take it with you, but I haven't heard of anyone who's ever come to Atlantis leaving, so knock yourself out." He smiled at me with the long piece of grass hanging from the corner of his mouth and I took a picture of the first somewhat-Atlantean person of the day. I was starting to feel giddy.

"I was celebrating my thirtieth birthday, it's 2010. I was scuba diving and a group of hammerhead sharks scared me so I cut the tag line to my partner. I was swept up in a current and knocked out. It was my first dive ever in the ocean, so I was taking as many pictures as I could. Would you like to see them?" I knew I was rambling but it wasn't every day I was able to talk to someone old enough to be my great grandfather; yet young enough to pass for my age. His eyes widened as I started to flip through the pictures on my underwater digital camera. I smiled as I watched his fascination with this piece of technology. If I remembered my history correctly, when he drowned, they were just starting to come out with color movies. He must've looked at every photo four times before shaking his head in amazement and returning it to me.

"They're truly masterful with their technology on the surface. I wonder how the people here will react to all the changes your culture's made. It's vastly different than seeing it in the reflecting pools."

"What are those?" I asked.

"They're less like pools and more like raised basins of water. There are two in Poseidon's temple. Atreyu helps me with the scrying. They are able to show you some of what's going on. They're like a mirror, but one that doesn't reflect; rather it can give a glimpse into a different place—as long as that place holds water. They remind me of the moving pictures from back home, but they seem fake there, just a bunch of pretense. I still think one of these days I'm going to wake up in a hospital back home and find that this was all a dream. The folks back home would never believe the magic here. Yours are probably even more jaded than my era was, what with all your advances in technology. In many ways though, Atlantis is still more advanced than this." He gestured to my camera and I raised an eyebrow in question.

"I have yet to see any form of technology here, aside from Raif's kitchen, but even the things in there seemed strange. They were modern appliances, but I don't remember hearing the hum of electricity or watching him actually turn anything on. There are no phones, cars, or televisions that I've seen; what is it that makes you more advanced?" I really wanted to know, I grew up with the myths and rumors of a highly evolved culture and it was killing me that these people appeared to be so archaic.

"We may not have the technology that you do, but we have this." He winked and then was gone—popped out of existence. I sat there with my mouth hanging open in surprise.

"Turn around, Natasha." I turned and he was leaning against a tree, pale with a sheen of sweat covering his face, laughing at me.

"How'd you do that?" I scrambled up and looked from where he had been to where he stood now.

"The Atlantean's use a higher percentage of their brains and can manipulate things. Each clan has different traits, but as I was delivered to the palace, I was meant to be mentored by an Atlantean from the royal family. I am, therefore, developing traits of those in the palace, even though Raifuku's been my teacher. I secretly wish I'd have landed in his clan, as his gifts are much more fun than teleportation. He keeps telling me that with time, patience, and practice I could do what the other clans do, albeit to a much lesser extent. He's able to teleport small distances and so is the priest, but I've just learned it and am trying to have fun with what I can do. You should see the look on your face. It's not as easy as it looks, but I do thank you for allowing me to show off." He smiled as he slid to the ground, his legs unable to hold him any longer.

"What can Raif do?" I resumed my position across from him, trying to hide how eager I was to know.

"You'll have to ask him. I'm not a person who tells tales that are not mine to tell." He was hesitant. "While I'd love to keep talking to you, you really should try to rest, you have a very long way to go tonight. When Raifuku sent me to watch over you, he told me of his plan. This may be a small island, but you'll be traveling to the other side, into the highest peaks. You'll be going slower than normal, since you'll be travelling in the dark. Raifuku cannot teleport you both there; and I fear that you don't have time to waste."

I looked at him questioningly. I knew I wasn't everyone's favorite person here, but I was staying on Raif's land—just as I'd been ordered to. It irked me to be ordered about, but it was so beautiful here, I'd tried not to think about it.

"King Nereus will have you killed even if everyone here wants you to live. He's never known a world outside the ocean walls. *Alma xemelga's* have been nothing to him but a fairy tale that's been told to him since birth. He knows of the history, but doesn't understand it, as he was only days old when Atlantis descended. He doesn't understand the need that all other Atlanteans have to find their mates, similar, in a way, to you and me. He watches the surface in the pools and sees the devastation Surface Dwellers have caused to each other. He's in no hurry to join lands that are perpetually in war."

"Why are you helping me then, if you know he wants me dead and you like it here so much?" My voice was soft; hiding the sliver of fear I held that he was manipulating me.

"I agree with Raifuku. His people were not meant to live in seclusion from the rest of the world. This land was meant to grow and evolve with the others, not maintain its stasis. The surface has suffered without Atlantis' input, just as Atlantis has suffered without the surface's influence. Atlantis needs to rise and remind the Surface Dwellers of the magic they lost and what the deep-seeded need is we all have but don't understand.

"Your people may have fun and have brief moments of joy, but they're not satisfied. I'm unsure they realize why that is, exactly. I had no idea that I was an incomplete person until I came here and discovered what was missing. My *alma xemelga* isn't here and I want to find her. I can't do that unless I'm able to see people outside of these lands. You'll find that there are others who are willing to help you as well. Take Atreyu, for example. He knows you and Raifuku are *alma xemelga.* He knows things that no other being could or should ever know. I have yet to figure out what his power base is, but I want to. He could've exposed the two of you, but he understands the necessity of returning to the surface, as well as the wisdom of not continuing to anger Poseidon. He'll delay your execution as long as he possibly can."

"What happens when Atlantis rises, and the rest of the world isn't ready for you?" I asked the question that had been nagging me since the first moment I learned of the prophecy.

"I have no idea. War, maybe? Or maybe it will be shocking enough to see an entire continent emerge from the sea that your people will be curious. That's not something even the reflecting pools can show." He tilted his head, hearing something I didn't.

"Raifuku returns, and I bid you farewell. May the gods bless you with clear skies and strong winds at your back."

With those parting words, he disappeared. I had a nagging feeling that I'd heard that somewhere before, but I couldn't place it. My thoughts drifted elsewhere as I watched Raif walk toward the house. He was carrying two packs that looked full. I took a picture before I ran through the back door of his house and jumped into his bed. He found me there minutes later as I pretended to be sleeping. His deep chuckle filled the room.

"No need to pretend, love, I saw you run to the house. It was a good thing I sent Michael to watch over you then, yes?" He climbed onto the bed and kissed me. It was as natural as breathing and I returned it with as much love.

He was heaven. Our kiss deepened with the passion that we'd both been holding back. He gathered me into his arms, smothering me in his warm embrace. I tore at his tunic, desperately trying to feel more of his glorious body pressed against mine. An eternity with him would never be enough.

He chuckled softly and helped me remove his shirt. My breath caught again at how physically powerful he was. His shoulders were wide and impressively built, with a strong torso. He was thick, tough, and very hard in all the right places. I felt one of my favorites pressed tightly against my thigh. I ran my hand down his chest and around his abs to his back where I gently scraped my nails up then harder down. His breath quickened to match my own.

He tore my dress down the middle, exposing my breasts to the air. My nipples were already pebbled in excitement, yet hardened even further at his groan of pleasure. He dipped his head and licked one. It was a soft lick that pulled a gasp from me. I threaded my fingers in his silky black hair, thrusting my breasts higher so he'd have better access to his feast.

He licked, suckled, and nibbled one breast until I thought I was going to explode from need. Then he started on the other and I was completely lost in a storm of feeling. I was wanton, a desperate woman needing only the satisfaction of his manhood thrusting deep into the very core of me. I whimpered and groaned, thrusting my pelvis up to him, praying he'd complete me.

I scored my nails down his back, careful not to break the skin. When I reached his pants I tore at the fabric, pulling and trying to rip them off as easily as he had torn my clothing from me. He released the nipple he was suckling on with a light pop and I whimpered at the loss of his talented mouth. I was rewarded moments later with him looking down on me, his eyes heavy with passion.

He grabbed my hands, placing them in his hair again. He leaned on one arm until his head was inches from my face and kissed me while removing his pants. My fists tightened in his hair, holding him as close to me as was physically possible.

The feel of his member, bare against my most sensitive area, brought a gasp from me that separated our kiss for just a moment. He slid back and forth against my wetness, rubbing my nub, until I seriously thought I might die. The pleasure was too much, yet not even close to what I so desperately craved. He had both hands in my hair, keeping our faces locked in a passionate embrace, so I brought one of mine down to explore him.

He was long and thick. My juices covered him, making it a slick surface to explore with my fingers. He groaned loudly, bringing his mouth down to my neck. I stroked him slowly, desperately trying to get him to match my suffering. I heard his quiet begging and guided his helpless thrusts to my entrance.

He felt the opening and we both gasped as he sheathed himself into my core. It hurt, but was quickly surpassed by the joyous feeling of finally being complete. We locked eyes from inches away as he slowly pulled out and pushed back into me. It was exquisite torture. I looked deep into his teal eyes until I relaxed, letting go of my insecurities at the love and desire I saw there. Deep in the very heart of my being, I knew this man would never hurt me.

He felt my walls drop, my body relaxing in his embrace. He kissed me and plunged himself into me over and over. The sounds of whimpering were quickly replaced with slaps of flesh and moans. I shattered into oblivion, screaming his name, my very essence exploding into the ether. He growled my name, holding himself as deep as he could, spilling his seed into the very core of my body.

I saw images of him as a boy, his life here, and the loneliness he'd felt until he saw me. I learned about him in those brief moments and I felt us starting to merge together. I could see the edges of my vision going black and threw up my emotional walls again. I didn't want to lose this connection with him, but I really didn't want to pass out. He rolled over onto his back, cradling me against his strong chest. I concentrated on hearing his heartbeat and almost missed what he was whispering.

"*My amada, eu te amo. A miña vida está completa. Ata o dus eu te amo.*" Over and over he whispered in his deep bass cadence. It was beautiful, though I didn't understand the words.

"I love you too, Raif," I whispered to his chest just before I fell asleep.

11

We left about an hour after the sun had completely set. I laughed quietly to myself because I still couldn't fathom how we could see the sunset when we were miles below the ocean and covered in water. I was dressed in one of Raif's old tunics and a pair of pants as he'd completely destroyed the dress that he'd had made for me. Pants were more practical for what we had planned anyway. I'd put my hair up in a bun under a really dorky looking hat at his insistence.

Raif was adamant that I attempt to look like an apprentice farm hand while we walked the main roads. I tried to point out that he was supposed to be at his house, guarding me, so it seemed rather pointless to hide who I was. Anyone we ran into on the way would know who I was because I was with him. He grunted a response under his breath that I pretended not to hear regarding women and their need to be correct all the time. I'd forgotten the fun parts of being in a very comfortable relationship, the teasing, the back and forth. I smiled. He swept me into his arms and kissed me.

"What was that for?" I said a little breathlessly.

"When a beautiful woman smiles at you, sometimes you just have to kiss her, especially when that beautiful woman is yours." He plopped me back down and I pretended to readjust my pack to hide my silly grin.

It seemed like he'd packed enough crap for us to camp for a week, not one night. His pack contained supplies; while mine held food and things we might need for the mating ritual. He wasn't all that certain of what we'd need and we were both hoping that Cleito would be better prepared.

He laced his fingers with mine as we walked in companionable silence. We were following the same path that we'd taken that led to the palace. He'd explained that we'd take this path to Melic, where we'd veer off onto a different, less traversed path to tromp through the woods and into the mountains. There was a hidden bridge there that we'd be crossing in order to reach the mainland of Atlantis. If all went well, we'd make camp in a cave tucked into the mountains on the mainland, just as the sun was rising.

After we'd been walking for a little while, I felt Raif tense next to me. The next moment I was being thrown into the forest, and he covered my body with his own. Three Atlanteans walked by us talking in a language I couldn't understand. They were obviously drunk and gesturing quite boldly. Raif's anger seemed to be increasing as they talked so I assumed they were talking about me.

"Hey," I whispered into his ear as loudly as I dared after they passed. "What are they saying, and why can I understand you, but not them?"

I put my hand on his cheek, gently forcing him to notice me and ignore the jerks walking toward his home. Even though I didn't understand them, I had a very good idea what they were planning on doing tonight. Why is it that in every culture, men's first response to a female threat was abuse? I suppressed my sudden anger and shivered. It was a good thing we'd left the house when we did. I didn't want Raif to feel it necessary to defend me against his people.

"They are saying things no woman should ever have to hear. Things I am appalled to have heard. Even if you were not my *amada*, I would still be taking you away from here happily. We must hurry. Once they realize we've left, they'll alert others. It's only a matter of time until someone realizes where we've gone." He tightened his grip on my hand, propelling me out of the forest. I thought he was ignoring the other part of my question, but after we'd put some distance between us and them, he glanced down at me.

"There is a natural translation that occurs when people visit Atlantis. It is part of the magic of the island. It happened when we were on the surface as well. When we had visitors, they would speak and hear things in their native tongue that would be automatically translated into ours for us and vice versa. It was very helpful for trading purposes to not have to learn all the foreign tongues. You do not understand certain things because I block the translation. I block it so you do not have to hear the things that those scumbags just said, but also so that you can understand some of my endearments in my native tongue."

"You don't have to protect me from what people say. I've probably heard worse said directly to me. Things aren't the same where I come from as they are here. Where I come from, women aren't treated delicately. We're treated just like men, sometimes worse. The era of gentlemanly behavior is long gone, requiring us to learn to defend ourselves. I've been alone for so long, I know how to defend my honor, if necessary. I know you may not believe me, as I gave in so willingly to you, but by now you should know our relationship is different and I wouldn't give of myself if I didn't want to. I'm flattered by your gallantry, but it's unnecessary." He frowned.

"That is one of the many things that I have concerns about with your culture. Women need to be protected and cherished. You are the giver of life and should never have to take life away. Men should do the things that are necessary to protect your delicate sensibilities. I have no doubts of your abilities, but you should not have this need. It pains me that I will not be able to protect you when you leave."

I actually felt his pain. It shot through my heart like a knife. It was very strange; feeling what someone else was feeling. I had enough problems keeping my own emotions under control; now having to add his into the mix was going to be a challenge. I held his hand tighter and knew that I'd distracted him enough with our conversation that he wouldn't worry so much about the repercussions from the men headed toward his home.

"Where are we going, again?" I whispered.

"There is a hidden bridge Poseidon built connecting Cleito's palace with Melic. Very few know of it as it's in an area even fewer venture to, and is older than many who live here. I found it by accident a few centuries ago, although I think perhaps it was less accident and more the will of Poseidon that guided me toward it. We'll have to be quiet until we get deeper into the mountains of Melic. I'm not sure if others will be out tonight." I nodded, squeezing his hand and trying not to be nervous.

I again felt Raif tense beside me as we approached the land bridge connecting us to Melic. He'd explained earlier that this would be one of our most vulnerable moments, as we were completely exposed and unable to hide. We'd have to cross as if we were not up to any mischief and hope we wouldn't run into anyone else. I felt his trepidation as we started walking. We were lucky that it was extremely dark here at night. It was so dark I couldn't see two feet in front of my face. His hand gripping mine was a lifesaver. The only way that we were going to be seen by anyone was if they walked directly into us. I forced myself to relax and sent the feeling of relaxed encouragement to Raif, or so I hoped.

Apparently, the gods were with us tonight, as we didn't encounter anyone else. Raif visibly relaxed once we were on Melic.

Veering off the old path onto a small deer trail, we made our way into the mountains where Poseidon's hidden bridge was.

I'd thought the night was dark before, but the farther we traveled into the inky blackness of the forest, the darker it became. It was filled with sounds of night animals out hunting and I was profoundly grateful for the strength of the man walking next to me. As brave as I tried to be, I still appreciated having his hand to hold. I looked at our intertwined hands, but couldn't even see them in the dark. I had no idea how he could see where he was going in the pitch black of the forest around us. When I asked, he just grunted and kept on walking.

"Is that just another magical trait of Atlanteans? You all have night vision? Michael told me about the gifts, so if you won't tell me if this is your talent, just tell me if anyone else can do this. I personally can't see a thing and am a bit freaked out by it." My unease released itself in its natural form of bitchy irritation. He slowed next to me and seemed to be gathering his thoughts. When he spoke, his voice was gravelly and rough like he'd been chewing rocks.

"It is the talent of my clan, though there are others who have the capabilities. It is difficult for me to speak while I am like this, but I will explain when we stop for food. We must hurry." I felt a sense of urgency, hiding a pang of regret from him so I muttered my thanks and continued on in silence.

We remained a quiet pair until we reached the foot of the mountains. The forest covered about a third of the mountain terrain, and we were going half that distance tonight. I had looked for the mountains when Raif was explaining our journey earlier, and was fooled into thinking that they weren't very ominous. They were steeper than they appeared from far off, and I was having difficulty, especially since I couldn't see a thing. It really irked me to struggle so much, but I never was much of a hiker. I had to cling to Raif's arm because I couldn't see, and was constantly tripping over things. I was beginning to think that it had been a mistake to attempt to navigate the mountain in the dark. With how thick the woods were and how remote the area was that we were in, no one would've seen us. I was beyond annoyed, and struggling for breath just to take another step.

He finally brought us to a stop, picked me up, and placed me on a boulder. My breath came in quick gasps and he was barely breathing hard at all. I felt out of shape and silly, so of course I bristled. I heard him walk away and I had to calm the panic that threatened to set in. I was alone in a strange place, ridiculously out of shape, and couldn't see a damn thing. I knew he wouldn't leave me, but the fear that had been barely restrained threatened to surface. Thankfully, he returned moments later with firewood. I heard a few whispered, guttural words and the logs lit.

It was peaceful sitting next to the small fire with Raif. We didn't need it for the warmth, but I had a feeling he was placating my need to see my surroundings. The noises of the forest had picked up around our small makeshift camp, and it was comforting to be able to see the space around us.

"I thought we couldn't stop until we reached the base of Cleito's castle? I can keep going," I said between gasps for breath. I didn't want to appear as out of shape as I felt. I'd almost finished my second canteen and forced myself to stop, knowing that we still had quite a ways to go. I couldn't even think about what all the liquid was going to do to my bladder.

"I know. I am hungry. I've also been debating with myself about something that I probably should have mentioned earlier. We will not make it to the base of Cleito's mountain at this pace." He brought his hand up at my objections. "It is not you, *amaáa*. I cannot make it to the base of her mountain like this and was not planning on it. I was waiting for the right moment to talk to you about this, but have been unsure of how to tell you. You mentioned that Michael shared his gift?" He looked surprisingly uncomfortable talking to me. I could feel how nervous he was, it was making the water I'd chugged sit uncomfortably in my stomach. I just nodded in confirmation, hoping he'd relax. "Well, at least this will not come as a complete surprise," he muttered almost to himself. "The only way for us to make it to the base of her mountain tonight is if I change and carry you."

"So, change. It's not as if I haven't seen you naked already. If it makes you feel better I'll turn my head." I was a tad insulted that he didn't want me to see him naked, but more confused as to why he was so upset about needing to wear something different. I still didn't see how this was a gift of his clan. Maybe he had magic clothing that he was going to put on. I snickered to myself at the thought of him wearing little sneakers with wings.

"I cannot explain further. It is draining to continue walking in my half state and even I cannot change too often or I will drain myself to the point of exhaustion. I will show you, but after we eat. I will be hungry after and refuse to hunt with you." He handed me some fruit and dried meat.

I was still lost, but entertained myself with the images of him flying about with winged shoes while we ate. He barely looked at me, but when he did, he looked almost as confused as I was. I guess my amusement at the situation appeared strange to him. Well, if he wasn't going to enlighten me on what he was hiding, I sure as hell wasn't going to share the nonsense pinging around my skull.

"Are you ready?" he asked when he was finished and had his pack secured loosely on his back.

"Yep, I just have to put my pack on. I really am capable of walking on my own, you know. I can try to go faster." He gathered me in his arms, searing me with a kiss.

"I know, *amada*, but it is not necessary. Even if we ran full out, we would not make it like we are. Please, trust me." His voice quavered. I kissed him and he gave me a very nervous smile. I had just a moment to wonder what would make him so afraid, when he started changing.

He was still holding me as it started and I could feel his muscles spasm. He fell to the ground, releasing me, and I heard the unmistakable sound of bones snapping. His skin rippled in the firelight. A slight whimper escaped, the only sign that it was more painful than he was letting on. It looked agonizing, but fascinating at the same time.

There was a moment where his body appeared to be just a mess of innards. I caught glimpses of bone, hair, and fur and I had a hard time making sense of what I was seeing. His helpless groan turned into a growl as his head reformed. Black fur sprouted over his entire body. It was over with quickly, faster than the old monster movies made it seem. He took a minute to breathe and to adjust to his new form before opening his eyes.

I found myself gazing into the teal eyes of my mate in the shape of a black leopard. I could still feel his worry that I wouldn't accept him, or that I'd now fear him, but he was so beautiful. I had to pinch myself to make sure it was real. He crouched down so I could climb up, keeping his posture low and as non-threatening as a leopard could, watching me warily. I didn't climb up straight away, instead leaning down to his level so I could pet the soft fur on top of his nose.

"So beautiful," I whispered, and he grunted in surprise. I walked around him, touching him and studying his muscular frame. I kneeled down taking his massive head in my hands and rubbed his ears. His eyes shuttered and he started to purr when I found a sweet spot right behind his ears.

"You silly man. You could've just told me about this. I don't think I'd have believed it until I saw it, but you could've told me. I hope there isn't anything else you've left out, or I'm going to have to kick your cute kitty butt." I smiled and tapped him on the nose. I stood and moved to put out the fire but stopped at his cough. "I'm just putting the fire out so we don't burn down the forest. I'll be right back." He shook his large black head no, so I shrugged, turned around, and climbed onto his back.

His pack was still around his strong shoulders, although more snug than before. There was room behind the pack for me to sit and cling to it.

Riding a leopard was right up there with one of the strangest things I'd ever done. I was deliriously happy to be riding on the back of a giant cat, and we took a few minutes to walk around the clearing to get our movements in synch. I had to get used to riding a leopard, and he was trying to adjust his movements with me attached to his back. I had a feeling that he'd never done this before. The third time we circled the fire I ended up on my backside in the dirt.

He tried projecting movements to me as feelings. When I finally picked up on that, I was able to adjust my body according to what he needed. We played in the clearing, while learning to ride together. He swatted at the leaves, leapt over the fire, and did figure eights to make certain that we were at ease with the various movements he'd perform.

When he finally felt comfortable with carrying me upon his back, he crouched up to the fire. I found my body mimicking his, crouching closer to his pack. He let out a kitty snort and I knew he was laughing at me. I smiled as he rounded the fire, and with his back paws, buried it.

I let out a snort of my own at the feel of his back paws scraping the dirt, followed by a squeal of excitement as he tore off into the woods. I held onto the pack for dear life, realizing now what he meant by us needing to travel faster. There was no way anyone could compete with this speed.

I felt trees and bushes scrape against my legs as he sped through the woods. I tried to keep my body plastered against his without squeezing his sides as he leapt over boulders, bounded over streams, and dodged plants and other animals. He didn't appear bothered in the slightest by the extra weight he was carrying on his back. He trusted me to follow his movements and I trusted him not to let me fall. As long as I didn't think about what was happening, we worked very well together.

He ran for what felt like hours, leaping across obstacles, dodging the ones he couldn't. I was just beginning to feel as though I couldn't hold on much longer when he began to slow down. The sky was just turning pink and I could finally see where we were. I was surprised to see that the forest had given way to a rocky terrain.

Raif's tongue flopped out of his mouth in a pant and he started walking. I slid off his back and started to search for another canteen in my pack. He let out a snort and growled at me in frustration, bumping his head against my butt, trying, I could only assume, to get me to continue on.

"Oh, stop it. You need to drink something and I need a break. We're almost there anyway, aren't we?" I opened my pack looking for the small pot he'd packed to cook with. He sat back on his haunches staring at me. I glanced up with my 'aha!' frozen on my lips and had to laugh. In front of me sat an enormous black leopard that was sitting patiently with a backpack on and his tongue hanging out, panting. His tail flicked as I poured water in the dish and gave it to him before the laughter got too bad.

I pulled out my camera as he drank and took his picture. He looked up at the flash and I took another one. He was beautiful. He tilted his head to the side in a puzzled expression. I'd forgotten to tell him about the camera. I thought about explaining it to him now, but simply shrugged—it was difficult to give explanations to a cat.

We walked side-by-side for another hour until we arrived at the bridge. I was expecting another large land bridge but instead found myself walking up to a rope bridge connecting our mountain to the next above a very deep gorge. I could see the water below, but it was just a small river from this altitude.

The bridge was ancient and didn't look as if it could hold a feather, let alone our combined weight. A breeze blew and the whole bridge swayed with it. I felt sick just looking at it.

"No. There's no freaking way I'm getting on that thing. We're just going to have to keep me hidden in your house. No one has to know we're mates. There's no way I am getting on that bridge." I crossed my arms and stared at him.

He huffed, and changed back into to himself. He was sweating, and had to lean against a rope post for support after his change.

"Natasha, it is perfectly safe. I will be with you the whole way. Come on." He pulled my hands apart and started leading me to the bridge. I felt my pulse in my throat. I couldn't do this.

"Please, Raif, can we find another way? I can't. I really cannot get on this thing." My shaky breath caught as he took a step out on the bridge. Panic flowed and I pulled against him. I couldn't get on that thing.

"See, nothing to worry about. We will be all right. I will hold your hand the whole time. Trust me." He moved farther out onto the swaying bridge.

"It's the bridge I don't trust, not you." He ignored my muttered response and began slowly crossing the rickety death trap. Our arms pulled as far as they could apart, and I made myself stare at his back as I took my first step onto the creaky old bridge.

He had one hand on the rope, while the other gripped mine. I let go of his hand in favor of curling my fingers into his pants so he'd have both hands free to guide and support us across.

I was momentarily distracted at the sight of my fingers clutching at his pants. *How did you keep your clothes when you changed?* The question was gone as quickly as it had come, overruled by another wave of fear as I glimpsed the distance between us and the bottom of the ravine. I closed my eyes, wishing I hadn't looked down. I kept them closed, preferring to put my trust entirely in Raif. We moved slowly, pausing only when the wind pushed us from side to side. I felt helpless tears leak out from my tightly closed eyes, my pulse thrumming quickly through my tense body.

I fell to my knees as soon as we were on solid ground again as my tightly wound muscles gave way to uncontrollable trembling. I felt him remove my pack from me and then heard his footsteps walking away. With the solid ground safely beneath my feet again, I couldn't bring myself to care about anything else. I crouched there, numb and shaking, ignoring the tears still falling down my face. He came back and picked me up from the ground. I felt bad for him having to carry me, but I was mostly just relieved to put more distance between that bridge and us. I opened my eyes finally to see where he was taking me. He walked into a shallow cave in the mountain and placed me on a pallet of blankets. He curled protectively around me, blocking my view of the bridge just past the cave's entrance.

"Not much for heights, are you?" His voice rumbled above my ear and I started laughing.

I laughed because he was right, because of the absurdity, and because if I didn't laugh at everything that'd happened since I'd boarded that stupid plane, I was going to cry. Again. He gave me a puzzled look but let me be hysterical.

I laughed until tears leaked from my eyes, bringing heaving sobs with them. I couldn't stop. The possible loss of my family, the loss of my naïveté, and the eventual loss of him was overwhelming. I didn't like crying, didn't like to feel the vulnerability, and that just made me cry harder. I cried and he held me until I finally, blessedly, passed out.

12

I woke hungry, sore, and embarrassed. He was still curled around me, his hand making a lazy trek up and down my back. His eyes were closed and he looked like he was asleep. I lay there for a few minutes admiring him, thankful that I'd discovered such an amazing person. I smiled at the memory of our ride through the woods and shifted so as to better see his features in the dim light of the cave. He cracked open an eye at my movement, rewarding me with a small smile of his own.

"Hey, I'm sorry about earlier," I croaked out, trying not to look into the teal eyes two inches from mine. I was mortified at having ugly-cried in front of him. "I'm not usually so emotional. Do we have any water left? My throat feels like sandpaper."

He kissed my nose and rolled me onto my back, still holding tightly to me so he was now on top of me. He reached over to his pack and pulled out a canteen, quickly rolling back over so I was on top of him. I sat, straddling him, drinking the water. He lay back, watching me.

"*Amada*, you never need to apologize for your tears. They are an expression of your feelings. I knew this would be a trying day, and you were amazing. With everything that has happened, I would have been surprised if you had not shed tears. I am pleased that Poseidon sent such a strong and wonderful woman here for me. I just wish that you did not have to leave. Are you feeling better now?" I'd finished drinking and was back in my favorite spot—pressed against his chest.

"Yes, I'm a little hungry, though. How long was I asleep? Did you eat yet?"

"Only for a few hours, and no I have not eaten yet. I did not want to disturb you. You needed the rest, we both did. We will eat now, and then we will have to head out. I am afraid you will like today's adventure even less than yesterday's." He grimaced as he stood to gather supplies. He had been going to my pack for the food this entire time, and had yet to open his own. It made me curious as to what he was carrying in the heavy looking bag.

"Don't tell me. More bridges?" I shuddered at the thought. I helped him get things prepared for the stew he was beginning to make.

"We are directly below Cleito's castle. The only way to get there from here is either teleportation, or climbing. I cannot teleport both of us such a long distance, as that is not my gift, so we will have to climb." He didn't look at me while he talked; subconsciously knowing that he wouldn't appreciate the glare I was giving him.

"Oh. I've never climbed the side of a mountain before. I should also tell you that I have this thing about heights." He turned, raising his brow at me. "I don't exactly like them." He smiled at my belated confession.

"Really, I had not noticed," he replied with a chuckle. "I have all of the equipment and can either buoy you to me like a backpack, or teach you how to climb, so you can climb with me. Either way, you will be near me and I will be happy." I bristled at the thought of him carrying me up the side of the mountain like an infant.

I stormed (limped; riding a leopard came at a price) out of the cave, and away from his laughter, before my pride got me into trouble. As I took in the mountain we'd have to climb, I rethought my earlier objection to being carried. It was forever, straight up. I couldn't even see a handhold to begin with, let alone how we'd climb the entire cliff-face. I walked back in with a more subdued attitude.

"I don't want to be carried, but I honestly don't know if I can do that. I've never climbed a mountain, and as you are now aware, I'm terrified of heights. I don't, however, want to be treated like a child. I'd like you to show me how, and if we have the luxury to take it at a speed that I can handle, I'll do my best. You said we'd be close the whole time, right?" I looked straight into his teal eyes, trying to be brave as I blatantly admitted my weakness. If he knew what that had cost me, he never showed it.

"I will be able to feel your lush body every step of the way. You are my heart, and I would never let anything happen to you." He smiled at me and I was glad I chose to learn and not be carried. This was a man who would cherish me, just as I was, even if I was afraid. However, I knew then that he'd respect courage more.

We ate in a comfortable silence, both contemplating the various aspects of the remaining journey. There are many things I'd done in the last day that I wouldn't have done for anyone but my *alma xemelga*. Without fully understanding it myself, I now realized that I'd been searching for a love to transcend time my entire life. There had to be a way for us to stay together. It wasn't fair that I'd find him, only to have to let him go.

I cleaned up while he went out to assess the mountain. He'd be starting our first few handholds so I could get the gist of it before we were too far off the ground. I tried not to think about it, I was already nervous. My pack was ready and resting in the cave's entrance. His open pack was already outside.

His pack was filled with rope, shoes, and gloves for both of us. I put my shoes on while he finished setting up the handholds. I pulled the rope and harnesses out of his pack and laid them out. I put my pack in his now empty one and waited for him to show me how to do this.

"We have enough light to make it to the castle by sunset, even if we go very slowly. Are you ready?" He looked excited. I wished I could share his enthusiasm, but I was just trying to keep our small meal in my churning stomach.

"Sure," I said, silently praising myself for not sounding as scared as I felt. I kissed him, deeply. "I love you."

"What was that for? Not that you ever have to have a reason to kiss me," he said as he smiled, with his arms wrapped around my waist.

"Just in case." I leaned into him, feeling his laughter rumbling deep in his chest.

"We will be fine, *amada*. I love you as well. Come." He led me to where I had put the gear, and demonstrated how to put the harness on.

I stepped into the leg holes of my rope harness and he drew it slowly up my legs. His hands barely held the rope as he slid them up the backs of my thighs, caressing the way to my butt. The heated look in his eyes made me forget momentarily what we were supposed to be doing, my heart pounded for another reason entirely. While I appreciated the distraction, I placed my hands on his, holding him still.

"You're incredibly distracting, but I really need to focus on what we're doing. This is terrifying to me, and doing that is just delaying the inevitable," I smiled.

He returned my smile, and obligingly began to explain that the shoes were helpful to grip the walls due to the orichalcum studs on the toes and bottom of the soles. He showed me how to release the handholds and jam them into the mountainside for maximum grip ability. He explained that the things I would know as called pitons were called esracador here. They were slightly different in structure than ours, though. They were created with orichalcum and embedded themselves into the crevices of the mountain, making themselves part of the mountain's structure, thereby creating a stronger, more stable hold. They worked by pressing the pointy end into the mountain and turning the handle one way. You turned the handle the other way to release the esracador in order to place it again.

He placed the esracador and climbed a few, to show me how to maneuver properly. I was very impressed with his skill, and debated again about the perks of being on his back while he climbed. He was graceful and skilled, shimmying up and down the mountainside like a lizard.

He had me use a few of the esracador to climb up, and I found that it wasn't that difficult. It took a surprising amount of concentration to place and remove them, and I didn't realize that I'd gone so far up until he told me to wait. It was actually sort of fun. I hung like a monkey on the side of the mountain and waited while he scurried back down to secure his pack to his body. I felt a little guilty that he was carrying both packs, but the guilt was quickly put to rest as I saw him clambering back up the mountain, gathering esracador on his way up like he was pulling taffy out of the wall.

He climbed up the side of the mountain to meet me with the speed and grace of a mountain lion, causing my mouth to both water and dry up at the same time. The esracador were clipped to his harness clinking together excitedly as he climbed. Once he reached me where I was clinging to the mountainside, he gave me a quick kiss before securing us together with a rope about three feet long. I appreciated the caution. He handed me half of the esracador so we could climb side-by-side. My reach was smaller than his, but we adjusted into an easy rhythm. It was easier than I'd originally thought, and before I knew it, we found ourselves talking about our lives.

I told him all about Ashlyn and Katie, sharing with him the love I had for them. He loved hearing about Ash and asked me all sorts of questions about her life and my role in it. He was amazed that Katie and I were able to handle so much without the aid of a man. I was starting to understand the culture he lived in, and I tried not to be insulted. I told him about my job, which further fascinated him. He couldn't fathom the idea that millions of tiny cells led to the construction of the body. We climbed in silence for a few minutes while he contemplated that.

"I was engaged once. His name was Keith and I thought he hung the moon." Raif tensed slightly next to me and my lips curved in a slight grin—he was jealous. I continued as if I hadn't noticed his reaction. "He left me before the wedding, I still have no idea why, exactly, but it broke something in me. I never thought I could love someone again; let alone think about committing my life to another person. But it's different with you."

As I reminisced about my relationship with Keith, I realized that it didn't have any depth to it. My hurt and anger toward Keith was finally nothing more than history to me. He truly was nothing more than a passing season in my life. I'd found my soul mate, my *alma xemelga*, and I was finally complete.

"With you, even with as short a time as we've known each other, I feel more complete than I ever thought I could feel. I'm content for the first time in my life. I guess I'd never really known love. Either that or finally finding my soul mate trumps everything. Because this should terrify me. And it doesn't. The only thing that scares me, that makes me question what we're doing, is the fact that I know I have to leave you." I was glad we had to concentrate on the wall. That way he couldn't see the vulnerability in my face, or the tears that threatened to fall at the thought of not being able to feel his touch whenever I wanted. It hurt to the very core of my being.

"*Amada*, I..." He paused for a moment. "*Ata o dus eu te amo.*" His voice was soft on the wind, but it filled my heart to bursting. I had no idea what he'd said, but I was beginning to understand that he would say things in his language that he thought might be too intense for me to believe just yet.

"Tell me about you," I demanded, changing the subject. "You've told me about your history and geography, but I know very little about you, and that's really the only subject that matters to me."

"I was born during a rich harvest. The only son to the Warrior Chief, the *Iochera* of my people, Mneseus, and his wife, Diana. Theirs was not a fairy tale love. They weren't soul mates, but I believe they loved each other as much as they were able to. I was still fairly young when Nereus was born—barely having seen my first century." I gasped. "Are you all right?"

"You're saying you were a hundred years old when Nereus was born, and that was *young?*" The astonishment in my voice was coupled with the look of shock I couldn't suppress. We paused in our climb, hanging against the cliff.

"I was 98 at the time of his birthing. I told you, we live for an extremely long time. By your standards, I would have only been in my early teens." It's one thing to know in a general way that someone is ancient, it's a completely different matter to listen to him talk about it as if it was no big deal.

"So, by your standard I'm still a child?" I curled my lip in disgust as thoughts rushed through my head, both good and bad.

"No," he replied with a grin. "If you were Atlantean, then yes, you would be a child, and wouldn't look as you do. We would not be able to mate—you would not have even come close to that age of possibility. Certain, um, things have to occur before that can happen." He actually blushed. I understood what he was trying to say; puberty had to happen in order to mate. That relieved most of my concerns. "We age at a much slower rate than you do. If I were a Surface Dweller, I wouldn't even have seen half a century yet. We are different from you, but in all the ways that matter, we are the same."

I nodded, not sure if I was entirely placated by his explanation, but not wanting to discuss it further and make myself more uncomfortable. I nodded, encouraging him to continue with his history.

"Mneseus was not an easy father. He raised me to both take over our place in the hierarchy and to take his place as the *Iochera* of Atlantis, should something ever happen to him. He was the one to lead the raid for Atlas—the one that left our city vulnerable to attack. My mother flung herself into the sea rather than face whatever retribution the gods had in store for my father's actions."

"Oh my god, Raif," I exclaimed in a horrified whisper. "I'm so sorry."

He gave me a sad smile. "Not necessary. It was a very long time ago, and I wasn't the only child to grow up before I was ready, or even to be left alone in this world. There were many who had it much worse than I."

"But still," I replied, "that had to be heartbreaking."

"Most of the families were destroyed in one way or another, either by the battle that led to our sinking or by Poseidon's rage after. If it weren't for Cleito, I believe that Atlantis would have been destroyed altogether. The orphaned children found homes with other clans. We went from a land home to thousands, to maybe a few hundred of us left. Almost all were in Nereus' palace when you were presented to him."

I wanted to say something, but didn't know what. It was horrifying to hear how an entire civilization was almost completely wiped out. There were only enough of them left to fill one—rather large—room. They were an endangered species, and my heart broke.

"I was lucky in a sense. I didn't have to rely on the others for survival. I was at the age where I'd have naturally started looking to be the man of my own home and leader of my clan. I became the *Iochera*. It was not a title I truly ever expected to attain, but I performed to the best of my abilities. Those few that would have named me friend quickly realized that I would uphold the laws of

Poseidon to the letter. They, along with a handful of women that failed to prove they could be my mate, dubbed me *xeada*." At my confused expression, he clarified with a grin. "Man without heart, or heart of ice."

"Why are you laughing?" I exclaimed. "That's a terrible name."

"*Amada*, if they could only see me with you, they would certainly know I was not filled with ice." I laughed at the passion in his voice, knowing he was right. "It was my job to train the remainder of our people in combat. I was also the administrator of punishments handed down by Nereus and Atreyu. Atreyu was kinder in his orders, he never asked me to do anything he wasn't willing to do, and he was always present. Nereus was more than content to order people beaten to the brink of death at the slightest provocation." He lowered his voice. "There is something not right with him."

I wanted to comfort him, to offer some solace against the horrors I knew he had to have committed over the centuries. The pain in his voice told me more than his words ever could. He shook his head as if clearing it from not-so-distant memories.

"There are a handful of people that have come here from the surface throughout the centuries, more so in more recent years. We're not sure how or why they are chosen to come, but each arrival brings a mixture of hope and terror. We're divided as a people; fear of being away for so long is fueling the dissent. While we all have a certain level of hope and desire to return to our rightful place amongst the Surface Dwellers, we fear the retaliation of your people." I bristled at his words.

"Your history has shown time and again that you are less inclined to accept that which is different. While we have grown to be a mostly peaceful society, there is no denying that we are vastly different from your people. I hope my people can return to their rightful place, that the reintroduction will go relatively smoothly, and that we will find a purpose in life again. We've been stagnant for so long, I don't even know if my people know of the wonderful things we could achieve alongside yours. We need to have the opportunity to find our mates, to belong to more than just this small island."

He was right. History had shown that we were capable of a lot of hatred and fear toward those different than us. We hadn't grown all that much, and I couldn't help but think that his people were right to fear rejection. For the first time since I'd met Nereus, I finally understood his reaction to me. I was a symbol of everything he could possibly lose. By fulfilling the prophecy, Raif and I were risking not only our life together, but also war between our people. It was a lot to process.

"When Michael arrived, he was the first person to see me as more than a *xeada* tool." He glanced at me. "Don't get me wrong, Atreyu never saw me as such either, he and Michael are the closest friends I have, but I still essentially worked for Atreyu. Michael was the first person who didn't want to use me, rather he wanted to learn from me and share experiences with me. He showed me that I could be both an enforcer and a friend. That those who truly cared would understand. He was a reminder to me that we have to return to our rightful place on the surface. And then you came." He was reaching for my hand. I hadn't realized we'd made it all the way up the mountainside, but there he was, leaning over the edge, waiting for me to join him. I placed my hand in his and he lifted me up effortlessly. I stood in his embrace, feeling a light tug of wind in my hair as he spoke.

"Your arrival changed me forever. Seeing you, vulnerable, unbreathing, limp in my arms, broke something inside me, and healed everything else. You complete and shatter me at once. And I wouldn't change that for the world. You are my *amada*."

"And you are mine."

13

Cleito's prison was an amazing castle carved intricately into the mountainside. I glanced down, still astounded that I'd made the climb without fear. Never in all my life had I imagined I'd ever scale the side of a cliff. I was giddy with excitement and glanced over at Raif whose smile matched mine. As spectacular as Cleito's castle was, it couldn't compare to the view of my love standing in front of me. I was still amazed that he was mine.

As he repacked all our climbing gear into his pack, I looked out at the whole of Atlantis. From this height, the poufy cloud cover hid most of the interlocking islands. Little specks of pristine water and green vegetation could be seen occasionally as the clouds moved in the breeze. It was like looking at the land from an airplane.

The most surreal part of it all, though, was the dome. We were so high that the clouds couldn't hide the luminescent sphere that I'd wanted to see since I arrived. It created the illusion of the sun's path across the sky. Currently, the dome was mimicking a westerly sunset. The colors winked in and out of existence, both on the dome and behind it. It was as if the sea itself had learned to mimic life closer to the surface as well. There were hundreds of sea creatures blinking in and out of sight past the sphere, their bioluminescence giving off the impression of hundreds of shooting stars.

I thought that eleven thousand years of this amazing view would almost be worth the imprisonment. There was a peacefulness here that I'd never experienced before. The majestic splendor made me reflect on the mundane nature of my previous life, the life I was destined to return to.

Raif's arms encircled me, holding me tightly in his embrace. His strong arms crossed protectively around my belly, making me feel safe and more loved than I'd ever felt before. He held me as if he were saying goodbye. I felt him tremble, so I turned to hold him close. It was a moment the poets have been striving to define in rhyme and song for an eternity. Some may have gotten close, depicting two lovers as the only two in existence, held in an embrace that would transcend time and space. Here, it was easy to believe that. Sadly, my thoughts strayed and reality came crashing in. This was not to last.

"This is the most beautiful thing I've ever seen. Are you sure that we have to do this? We could stay here, locked away with Cleito for the rest of our lives," I whispered softly to him, silently praying he would agree to this suggestion. The longer I was with him, the less I wanted to be anywhere else. There were tears in his eyes as he shook his head. I sighed, turning my head so he wouldn't see the tears gathering in my own eyes. I stood quietly in the shelter of his arms for another few minutes, just trying to enjoy the moment. We wouldn't have many more.

"Well, we'd better start looking for Cleito, then." I pulled from his embrace, knowing if I didn't, I'd never find the strength to pull away again. We put our packs back on and I clutched his hand. Together we walked toward what I could only imagine was the most spectacular prison ever created.

"It has taken you quite long enough to get here. Do you realize how difficult you have made things for me?" At the sound of Atreyu's voice, Raif's strong arms pulled me tightly to his side.

"Atreyu, what brings you here?" Raif was having difficulty controlling his features; the fear in his voice was plainly evident.

"Helping you, of course, you hard headed fool! I knew from the moment you walked into the king's castle that you two had mated. It was obvious to any who chose to look. You have rarely willingly touched another person before her, Raifuku." His tone softened. "This is the right course to take, even if Nereus objects. We were not meant to live under the seas. There is much to learn and discover on the surface. We should have adapted thousands of years ago, evolving with the humans. Instead we've been stuck watching the things they do while we maintain the old ways. I also do not wish to face Poseidon's wrath again. He must be allowed to reunite with Cleito or we, as a people, will be eliminated. We must also be allowed to find our mates." This last statement was said softly as if he were trying to hide the pain lacing his words. "There are wards placed upon the castle preventing any from entering, and Cleito from leaving. I have worked them before and will hold them so that you may enter." He strode forward, not expecting or wanting a response from us.

His arms extended, and a wind picked up from nowhere, whipping at his robe. His hair danced about his head in a silvery mass that looked like fire. I dwelled for a moment on the pain in his voice when he mentioned finding a mate. I pushed all other thought aside, however, as he led us into Cleito's castle.

INTRICATE CARVINGS lined the entryway of the castle. It was as beautiful as it was foreboding. Atreyu navigated the halls, twisting and winding until I knew I was utterly lost. My grip on Raif's hand was almost as tight as his grip on mine. All I could hope was that

Atreyu was truly a friend, and was taking us to Cleito. The darkened halls lightened abruptly as we rounded yet another curve. It opened into a vast garden filled with vibrant plants. We were in the heart of her palace, the mountain jutting up around us. Flowers in every shade and shape bloomed everywhere you looked, their pungent odor stimulating the body and mind. There were trees and bushes lining the walkway, and wildlife walked about as if we were out in the wilderness. There were garden walls surrounding us, and in the center of it all was a very plain, very ordinary, circular stone fountain.

Cleito was sitting on a bench at the side of the fountain, waiting for us. She was still as young and as beautiful as the statue I saw of her only two days prior. Her waist length golden tresses were held away from her face with intricate interlocking braids that looked impossible. She turned to face us and I smiled.

She personified beauty—her crystal blue eyes appeared large on her pixy face. She was petite and delicate, like a porcelain doll. She looked at me and for a moment the pain in those blue depths spoke her true age, reminding me of what I was soon to face. She stood to greet us.

"Welcome, my children. Your road has been long and difficult, and it will be more so before this day is complete. Please come and be welcome." Her voice was like the tinkling of bells caressed by the wind.

I had the urge to hug her, so that's what I did. I wrapped my arms around her tiny frame and drew her to me. Raif gasped behind me as he and Atreyu kneeled in supplication, his body tense, radiating emotions I couldn't decipher.

"I'm sorry. I probably shouldn't have done that. You just looked like you could use a hug. I'm Natasha. I still don't quite understand your customs." I smiled uncomfortably; afraid I may have insulted her.

"Do not fret my child." She squeezed my arms as she moved past me to stand before the men kneeling at her feet. Her hand trailed through Atreyu's silver hair. "Atreyu, please get off your knees. Raifuku, gather your mate and follow me. There is much to be done if we are going to do this properly. You must complete the mating ritual and be bound in mind, body, and spirit before you can separate, or it will not be effective. I have everything prepared; I have just been waiting for you. I trust you have the gown and the rings?" At Raif's confused look she sighed. "It doesn't matter, I have Atlas' old rings, and I think Merick's wife was about your size, although not quite so voluptuous. It will have to do."

"Mistress, forgive me, but I am having Michael bring a dress to suit our needs as well as something for Raifuku. He is also needed for a witness. The ceremony is incomplete unless there are two to bear witness. I had hoped he would be here by now, but he may be having difficulty teleporting the distance. I shall discover what keeps him and return shortly." Atreyu bowed formally and left.

Cleito sighed. I caught a hint of disappointment as she gazed at Atreyu's departing figure. She led us through another maze of rooms and halls, into separate chambers to wash up before the ceremony. My room was amazing. There was a large, four-poster bed in the middle, complete with a canopy. It was done in various shades of purple that would normally make me feel like the Easter Bunny had exploded, but here it appeared elegantly.

The walls were a dark purple, accenting the lavender canopy covering the bed. The carpet was a very deep brown, almost the same color as the furniture. There was a vanity, complete with an antique silver dressing set, across the room from the bed. The mirror glittered from the soft candlelight flickering everywhere. Next to where I stood in the doorway, was a small chest of drawers with another mirror. All the mirrors in the room multiplied the few candles that were lit until the whole room seemed to be flickering and dancing with candlelight. The decor was like something out of a history book and I caught myself chuckling at that thought. It looked like it came straight from a history book because it sort of did. It was ancient. Everything here was ancient, including my mate.

I was growing more and more nervous as time passed. I hadn't been expecting the mating ceremony to be as big an ordeal as it was turning out to be. I still had no idea what to expect. For some reason, I'd just thought we had to have sex. I should've asked Raif what the protocol was when I had the chance. Not that it would have changed anything. I just would've liked to have a better understanding about what was going on and what was about to happen. I was starting to feel like I was only getting snippets of information and only when absolutely necessary.

The bathroom was through an archway across from the room's entrance and was just as opulent as the bedroom. I bathed in the deep, claw-footed tub that was in the corner of the bathroom and felt like a princess. The bath was filled with herbs that released a calming aroma into the air. More herbs were burning from incense holders hanging around the room. The scents of lavender, vanilla, and eucalyptus filled my nose, relaxing my muscles slowly. I was half asleep in the warm waters when Cleito entered carrying an armful of scarlet fabric. She laid it on the bed and came over to help me prepare.

"Atreyu has returned with Michael. They are assisting Raifuku, as well as making the final preparations for the ceremony. Let us work on you, shall we?" Everything she said was delivered with an air of dignity and grace.

"May I ask you something?" I said as I finished drying.

"I will answer what I am able." She sat me in a chair and started brushing out the tangles in my hair.

"What does this mating ritual consist of? I probably should've asked Raif earlier, but it just didn't seem to matter. It still doesn't, but I don't know how comfortable I'll be with people watching the event." My face turned about the shade of the dress that Cleito had brought and I fought the urge to look away. I didn't think I should be embarrassed about something as wonderful as becoming one with my soul mate, but the thought of people watching us have sex made me profoundly uncomfortable. And if that's what this mating thing consisted of, I wasn't entirely sure I could go through with it. It also struck me as odd that we'd need an audience at all—we'd already had sex, wasn't that good enough? She smiled at me, as if she could hear my internal struggle.

"Oh, you are precious! You can do that part privately, after you have been handfasted. Handfasting is an ancient tradition binding two people in this life and beyond. It is the outward, physical manifestation of your soul's intent. You are being prepared for your mate as I was for Poseidon. You must be bound to Raifuku body and soul to complete the *alma se funden*."

"I've heard of handfasting before. Isn't it just a trial marriage?" I asked, remembering some obscure bit of information I'd picked up from somewhere years ago.

"Sadly, like so many things, it has become so much less on the surface." Cleito lowered her head. "Handfasting is even more ancient and meaningful than your histories tell. While I know you feel as if you are already bound, there are still rituals that must be performed, and you must be blessed by the lord and lady. They are older than even the oldest gods and must bless your union before you can be complete." She was skillfully plaiting my hair into intricate braids around my head as she spoke.

"Oh, so it's like a marriage." Surprisingly, I wasn't terrified at the thought. I had realized as Raif and I were making our way to Cleito's palace that I'd do anything to be with Raif. He truly was the other half of me, fulfilling me in ways I'd never thought possible. When we were together, I no longer felt empty, but joyously complete.

"It is similar, yes, but not entirely the same. Our handfasting is more permanent than your common marriage. It cannot be broken by a mere piece of paper or by death. It forever binds your heart, body, mind, and souls together as one. It brings us back to how we were first created, before the first soul's division. You have accepted the fact that after you mate, you must separate from each other, yes?" Her hands stilled for a moment as she asked the question.

"Yes, he told me about the prophecy and what we'd have to do." Her hands picked up their work once more. "The thought of leaving Raif tears me apart, but it'll set things right with your people, and I'll see him again someday. Knowing he's here, feeling him in my heart, that will be enough until the day I can be with him again physically." I smiled and hoped it was convincing. I really didn't want to lose him, even for a moment. I had no idea how she'd lived for so long without Poseidon.

She opened her mouth as if to respond, but then shut it again. She looked conflicted about something, and I looked up at her, encouraging her to continue. She wasn't given the opportunity, however. A knock at the door interrupted our moment.

"Forgive me, but we must hurry before my absence is noticed." Atreyu called from behind the closed door. "King Nereus is determined to see Natasha eliminated before she finds her *alma xemelga* and fulfills the prophecy. We will be waiting." His footsteps were fading away before either of us could form a response.

14

I felt beautiful. The scarlet dress molded to my body like a second skin from my chest to my waist. The skirt billowed out from my waist down, swaying with each step I took toward my future. My auburn hair was held away from my face in a series of intricate braids and knots, leaving most of it to flow down my back. I couldn't imagine a more perfect day than today, and wouldn't ruin it with thoughts of what would happen later. I was binding with my soul mate, and nothing could compare to this moment.

I rounded the corner behind Cleito and saw the clearing. There was a circle enclosed by orichalcum stones in front of a forest. Cleito explained that this was the same location that she and Poseidon had their handfasting, as well as where the curse occurred.

It was beautiful, as was the man waiting for me. He was covered head to toe in black. His eyes shone with such love for me, I thought my heart would burst right then.

He took my hand as I approached him, and the ceremony began. Cleito and Michael stood with us as our witnesses and Atreyu performed the rights, as was his duty. He rang a small silver bell three times. Raif began to walk around the circle, and I followed his lead. We then entered and stood facing each other in front of an altar. Atreyu prompted us to state our intent and Raif started.

"I, Raifuku Iochera, have come of my own free will, in perfect love and perfect trust to bind myself completely from now until the end of days to my *alma xemelga*, Natasha."

"I, Natasha James, have come of my own free will, in perfect love and perfect trust to bind myself completely from now until the end of days to my soul mate, Raifuku." I was so overjoyed; I barely noticed the twin tears sliding down my face or the misty rain that had begun to fall. Atreyu rang the bell.

We exchanged rings as a sign to the outside world of our commitment to each other. The palms on our left hands were cut, and the blood dripped into a chalice that was half filled with wine. Our hands were then bound together, mixing our blood. I was slightly unnerved by this, but tried to remember that it was part of their culture. We used our right hands to drink from the chalice, symbolizing the need for balance between being together and apart as well as infusing our bodies further with the essence of each other.

Our right hands were then placed over our left ones and tied tightly together. We repeated our intent to be bound for the rest of eternity. Atreyu rang the bell.

We sealed our intent with a kiss. The knot was undone, and we each cut a lock of hair from the other and placed it into a silver box. As we buried the box at the foot of the altar we repeated our intent to be bound again.

"Thrice called, thrice answered, the souls are now combined. In perfect love and perfect trust, they remain until the end of time. So mote it be." Atreyu's words rang out and a shiver ran down my spine. A hush fell over us.

The birds stopped singing; it was as if the entire universe was holding its collective breath at this moment. We walked around the circle again, the opposite way, sealing our vows with a kiss as we ended. The ground rumbled beneath us. We'd completed the first a*lma se funden* in Atlantis in over eleven thousand years.

We celebrated with Cleito, Atreyu, and Michael in Cleito's palace. We had a small feast, with pleasant company. Atreyu tended to the small wounds on our hands, somehow reducing them to thin red lines.

"That's crazy," I whispered, fully examining the cut made earlier.

"You are mated to an Atlantean. Your body will go through changes now," Atreyu explained. "You are no longer just human. You will age differently, heal differently, and may take up other traits of your mate." He smiled. Rain gently sprinkled down upon us. Atreyu glanced at Cleito who was sitting just out of earshot of us. She looked euphoric, but unshed tears made her eyes bright in the candlelight.

"She is the most caring soul I have ever known. If she were able to shed tears, she would for the simple joy of bringing a soul together again. Poseidon sheds them for her." Atreyu gestured to the sky. "He shares her joy that they will soon be reunited." Atreyu loved Cleito. It was clear in the way he spoke about her; as though she were the most precious being in the world.

"There is one more ritual you must perform before you return to the surface." Atreyu interrupted my inner musings. "You must return Cleito's tears to her."

"How?"

"I honestly have no idea." Atreyu had the decency to look embarrassed. "The fates will guide you, show you the proper way."

"Yeah, right," I whispered under my breath. I wandered away from Atreyu, leaving him to gaze at Cleito longingly. After we'd celebrated with each other for a little while longer, the men left to congratulate Raif, praise Poseidon, and whatever else it is that men do at a handfasting, leaving Cleito alone with me.

"I think this is as good a time as any to give you my tears, is it painful?" I was more nervous about this than I had been about my handfasting. I hadn't processed any of what was happening yet. It all still felt like a very strange dream.

"No, it is not painful. It is strange, though, to cry without shedding tears. I believe you must first begin to cry, and then simply give them to me. Your sacrifice will be remembered for years to come. I know better than most how much all of this is costing you." She looked very sad and the rain came down stronger. I thought of sad things and attempted to cry. I smiled apologetically at Cleito when nothing happened.

I forced my thoughts to wander to what life would be like without Raif in it, without seeing his dimpled smile, hearing his deep bass voice, or being able to hold him in my arms. I felt the tears begin to slide down my cheeks almost immediately as the pain of being apart from him hit me completely for the first time. I didn't want to stop the last tears I'd ever shed, so I stood there for a minute, letting them fall, paying homage to the love I was leaving. When they started to slow, I gently scooped one from my cheek and placed it against Cleito's eyelids.

"I freely give of my tears," I whispered, not knowing why, but feeling it was the right thing to say. In an instant, her cheeks were wet, the rain stopped, and so did the flow of tears from my eyes. It truly was a strange feeling to be sad and want to cry, but to be utterly unable to do so.

"Bless you, child. You and Raifuku must say farewell. Enjoy every moment with him, but don't take too long. I shudder to think what Nereus will do if he finds you here. You will always be cherished in my heart." She kissed my forehead and walked away. I went into my room to wait for Raif.

HE WAS already waiting for me on the bed when I walked through the door. He'd taken his shirt off and was sitting there in his black pants with his head in his hands. He looked miserable. It wasn't a look I'd anticipated on my wedding day from any man, especially my soul mate.

Seeing him there was bittersweet. I was overjoyed to have him in my life for however brief an interlude, but extremely depressed knowing we'd be apart after tonight. I hoped to spend the rest of this night forgetting I was leaving in the morning.

"Don't look so happy to see me," I whispered as I shut the door. His head jerked up in surprise before he thought to school his features. His eyes were swimming with unshed tears. He blinked them back so I wouldn't notice, but it was already too late.

"Oh, Raif, I don't know what to do. I love you so much it hurts. Seeing you like this breaks my heart. We'll see each other again someday. Don't cry yet. I'm still here, hold me while you can. Please, don't cry," I said, tears I would never shed, choking my voice.

I flung myself onto his lap hugging his torso close to my cheek. If I'd still had tears, I'd be crying with him. There had to be another way. It just wasn't fair. He stroked my hair while my head lay in his lap.

I nestled closer to him, curling my body around his legs. We sat in silence for a while, just holding each other. I ran my hands in gentle circles around his lower back, hoping to ease his pain just a little bit. At this moment, I really didn't care about the gods or the culture of a people I knew nothing about, all I cared for in this world was the man trembling beneath my palms.

"Natasha, forgive me. I cannot seem to forget that you will be gone from me tomorrow. I am not ready to lose you. Even if we'd spent eternity together, I would not be willing to give you up yet. You truly are my other half and it is painful to know that I will be without you again. It was not so difficult before I knew you, but now it is as if Zeus himself has placed a lightning rod in my heart." He tilted my chin so I was looking into his teal eyes.

The love and pain in those depths tore at my heart. This man truly loved me. I lifted myself very slowly from my crouched position and brought my lips toward his, never losing eye contact. He blinked just as our lips met in the chastest of kisses and twin tears spilled down his cheeks.

"Don't cry, *amada*. I'm here," I whispered against his mouth. I kissed the tear tracks from his cheeks. I kissed each of his eyelids. I kissed his mouth a few more times, very lightly. They were chaste, virginal, kisses. I wanted to cherish this moment for as long as possible. I pulled back, bringing my hands up to caress his face. He was such a strong man it tore at me to see him so sad. "I love you," I whispered as I cradled his cheeks in my palms and kissed him like I'd wanted to all day. I kissed him as if I couldn't get enough of him, because I couldn't. I held his face immobile and devoured him. His eyes flew open in surprise at the first intense contact and he kissed me back with every ounce of passion he felt. He moaned in my mouth, his strong hands roving across my back to lift me onto his lap.

I pulled away, breathless. I wanted this, but I wanted it slowly. We had the entire night to worship each other and I didn't want to waste it. I also vainly didn't want him ruining yet another dress. I was rather fond of this one. It was, after all, the dress I'd gotten married in.

Holy crap, I'm married.

I felt the color drain from my face as it finally hit me. What timing. I was about to make love to the most incredible man on the planet, and that's when I decided to freak out about the fact that the man was my husband. Why couldn't this have happened earlier in the day, preferably when I was alone? I swallowed, trying to moisten my suddenly dry throat, and sat heavily against him on the bed.

"Natasha, what is the matter? Have I done something wrong?" He took my hands in his; forcing me to look at either his face or our matching rings. I chose his face as the rings had me hyperventilating.

"We were married today," I said, my voice shaking. He smiled at me.

"Yes, that is part of mating. I thought every woman dreamt of this day from childhood. Does it bother you?"

"I just never planned on getting married. It was never something I wanted, and now that it's happened, I'm not sure how I feel about it." I wanted him, but since Keith, I had never envisioned myself as a bride.

"*Amada*, do you love me?"

"Of course, I do."

"Then what does a ceremony matter? It is tradition for my people to assist the souls in the merge, nothing more. We already started to merge the last time we were intimate together. I know you felt it. Cleito insists that we must do everything as she and Poseidon did in order to properly break the curse on our people. I don't believe all that was necessary, but when dealing with the fates, it is better to be overly cautious. Does it bother you to be married to me?"

"What? No! I love you, and know that I want to be with you for the rest of my life. I'm being silly. I guess I just didn't expect this." I looked down at our intertwined hands. Circling his finger was a band made of orichalcum with a vine carved around it, and mine bore the match. The only addition to mine was a small opal in the center. I smiled, remembering that opals were his favorite stone.

I shook my head as if that movement would help me clear it. I was married. To an amazing man that by all rights shouldn't even exist. I smiled at my foolishness, sobering quickly as I remembered I would need to leave all too soon.

"Is there any way that I can stay, that I don't have to leave?"

"No. Unfortunately the oracle decreed that we must willingly separate to reunite our people. I wish there was another way as well.

I will miss you dearly." I snuggled closer to him, resting my head against his heart, listening to the beat. We sat in silence for a few minutes, simply holding each other.

"I'll miss you as well," I whispered. I stood up and removed my dress, placing it in the corner of the room. I walked back to him, completely nude and not the least bit self-conscious. It was hard to feel insecure when he was looking at me like I was to be his last meal. A slow, seductive grin spread across my face as I reveled in his adoration.

"Love me, *amada*," I said as I pressed him onto the bed.

I was bolder than I'd ever been in my life. Straddling my legs on either side of his hips, I licked a path slowly up his abdomen to his chest. I stopped for a bite at his nipples, suckling on them as he'd done to me before.

He groaned, fisting his hands in my hair, struggling to let me control his torture. I licked his pebbled nipple, then blew across it causing him to shiver. I felt myself growing wet with the knowledge that I alone held the power to make this strong man beg. I flicked his lonely nipple gently with the tip of my finger and felt him buckle beneath me. We both groaned. I was having a very hard time keeping things slow as I could feel myself throbbing with need. My core craved to have him where he belonged, as did the rest of my body.

I moved my attention from his nipples to his neck, where I nipped him with my teeth. He started to pant. I nibbled on his earlobe just as his hands found my breasts. His fingers brushed my pebbled buds, causing me to contract on top of him. I moaned against his neck, praying he'd apply pressure.

When he did, I lost all pretense of going slow and kissed him. I ravished his mouth, kissing and biting his lips. I was controlled only by need. He kissed me back just as urgently, still maintaining his torturous caress of my breasts. I brushed my core against his member, still enclosed behind his pants, and came. It was a small release, but opened me to him in ways I hadn't experienced before.

I began to feel what he must have been feeling this whole time. It was like being one person with two bodies. The feelings intensified to where I could literally feel what I was doing to him. I heard his thoughts at a distance. We were finally fully completing the *alma se funden,* the soul merge.

We turned so he was on top of me, crushing my breasts in his palms. I was in ecstasy. He moved from me for a second to remove his pants and I heard someone whimper. I was slightly appalled to realize it was me. All was forgotten two seconds later at the look of pure male satisfaction on his face. He knew he had the same effect on me as I did on him and it made him very happy.

He scanned my body from head to toe, then his gaze lingered on my breasts. I knew what he was going to do seconds before he did it. Even if I couldn't feel him in my head, it was written in the expression on his face. He dove at my nipples, taking time to fully arouse and torture each one properly.

My hands fisted in his hair and I begged for any type of release. The sensations were too much for my sensitive skin. He kept his bottom half just far enough away from me so I couldn't find release by rubbing against him. I was like a cat in heat. I heard myself begging him, pleading with him to enter me. I needed him inside me more than I needed my next breath. He relaxed his assault on my breasts and held himself immobile, inches from my body. It took me a full minute to focus on his face, inches away from me.

"Look at me." He was as breathless as me, but firm in his demands. I forced my eyes open to look into his passion filled teal ones.

He slid into me and it was a struggle to keep my eyes open. He wanted me open to him in every way. He tried to be slow and gentle. I could feel his intent, although it was pointless since I was bucking beneath him. I needed him desperately. I gripped his shoulders, thrusting my pelvis along his shaft. I leaned my head forward to kiss him, but he held himself completely immobile.

"Kiss me," I whispered, and he finally capitulated. He kissed me deeply, almost bruising my lips with his hunger. My nails scrapped down his back in the ecstasy of impending release. He pounded into my wet core, sliding in with ease. It was no longer a painful coupling as it had been the previous times, but a glorious act of mating between lovers. I matched him thrust for thrust, feeling my body work its way to that final precipice. I felt my shields start to rise and he stopped.

"No, look at me. Let me in. Let me love you." He waited until I relaxed again to start moving inside me. I kept my eyes open, concentrating on his. I distantly felt the pleasure building, but forced myself to concentrate on Raif. I loved him and wanted him more than anything. He was completely open to me, letting me feel what he felt, hear his thoughts, and know everything about him. I was the one holding back.

I forced myself to relax in his embrace, loving him as he loved me. The orgasm came as a surprise to me, splitting me into a million pieces. I was completely open to him, vulnerable in a way that I'd never allowed myself to be. He came seconds after, causing my body to continue to react in bliss.

Subconsciously I saw an image of our souls. Each was broken, not split in half, but more like Swiss cheese. They were iridescent shadows of us with parts missing. Each part that I was missing, his soul had, and each part his was missing, mine held. In my euphoric dream state, I watched as the two souls slammed together, becoming one beautiful bright being. It hurt my eyes to look upon the incandescent beauty of our soul, and I had to look away. I opened my eyes, gasping for breath as I did so, not realizing I'd been holding it. I looked into Raif's eyes and saw a similar expression of awe reflected in his face.

"Did you see that too?" I breathed. He simply nodded. "That was amazing. Do you feel different? I feel fuller, but stretched, like I'm trying to fill two places."

"I feel you," he whispered in awe. "I feel what you feel. I can feel an echo of your heartbeat next to mine. Your emotions are intense. I had no idea it'd be like this."

He drew me into an embrace, holding me tightly to his chest. We lay curled up in each other's arms, just listening and feeling all the new things our mating brought about. I was more content and peaceful than I'd ever been in my life. This was the way we were meant to be. If I'd had doubts before this night, they were all wiped away with our joining. There really was such a thing as soul mates, and I was beyond blessed to have finally found mine. We drifted off to sleep with inconceivable love in our hearts and contented smiles on our faces.

I WOKE a few hours later with the sunrise. I'd never been one to sleep long, and was content just watching Raif sleep for a while. He was an amazing man and I wanted to remember this moment. I crept out of bed to grab my camera. It was still in my bag, but not in the place I'd left it, which struck me as strange. Raif must've moved it when he was looking for something.

I made my way back to the bed and took a few pictures of him sleeping. I wanted to see him at least in my photos if I couldn't see him in person. I was going to have to wake him soon so we could say goodbye, but I really didn't want to. I moved to sit back against my pillows to review the pictures I'd just taken and noticed that the battery was low.

I hadn't used it that much, so I ran through all the photos on the memory card to find out why. It appeared that Michael had confiscated my camera and taken pictures of the handfasting yesterday. The entire day was immortalized on film. If I'd had tears, my eyes would be welling up. This was the greatest gift anyone could've given me. I saved a few of the pictures from the memory card to the camera's limited hard drive, and then removed the memory card. I put the camera back into the bag that Raif would be taking home with him. I wanted Raif to be able to see me whenever he wanted.

I put the same red dress back on and slipped the memory card between the fabric and my breasts for safekeeping. I made sure the card was hidden, where no one could see it and went back over to the bed. I crawled in beside Raif, curling against his body. Gently I stroked the black hair from his face; admiring him. His lips curved up in a smile as he slept.

"Raif, *amada*, love, wake up. I have to go." I didn't want to leave. I really, *really* didn't want to part from him. My heart clenched at the thought and he frowned. He gathered me in his arms and finally opened his sleepy, teal eyes.

"What is wrong, my heart? You are so sad." He yawned before realizing I was fully dressed. Clearly the night of pleasure had wiped the morning of imminent pain from his mind. I saw the moment that he remembered and could feel his anguish.

"You are ready, then?" he whispered.

"Never. I'll never be ready or willing to leave you. I know it's what we must do, and if I wait any longer, I won't be able to go through with it. I have to go now. I just wanted to say goodbye. Do you want to walk me to the portal, or just stay here?" I wasn't entirely sure if I wanted him there. I couldn't be sure that I wouldn't back out at the last minute if he were standing there, staring at me with his sad eyes. Of course, if he didn't come to see me off I would have been heartbroken. Stupid female emotions.

"I feel your torment," he said with a hint of a smile on his face. He sobered quickly, though. "I will go with you and watch you leave to make sure you are safe. I will not ask you to stay with me, and I will not make it harder for you to go. But I do not want you to think for one minute that I want you to go. What we are doing is bigger than us, more important than our desires, and we shall be rewarded for our sacrifice. I love you with every fiber of my being, please never forget that."

He held me close. I could feel the tears slide down his cheeks, the pain in his heart, and the truth of his words. I loved him equally. We cuddled for another few minutes, both reluctant to let go of each other. Finally, though, we did part, knowing if we didn't now, we wouldn't be able to muster the courage to do so later. He dressed quickly and together we walked to Cleito's garden.

She was waiting for us in the same spot as yesterday. Atreyu was sitting with her, holding her hand. I could tell there was a story between them. I wouldn't be the one to pry it from them, yet I felt pity for Atreyu. He would be the one to suffer once Poseidon returned to his mate. They turned as one to look at us, quickly releasing the hold they had on each other's hand.

"Are you both certain you want to do this? You must be completely willing for the spell to work. It has never been done before, and it must be followed exactly. I will not fail my people again." Cleito was fierce in her conviction, a mother defending her young.

"We're sure. Let's get this over with. What do I have to do?" My heart thundered in my chest. Raif squeezed my hand in support.

"Simply step into the fountain and walk out the other side," Atreyu said. "You will be transported back to the surface immediately. I do not know where, and I do not know how much time will have passed since you left, but Poseidon will attempt to direct you close to your people without losing much time. He owes you that much," Atreyu spoke with conviction, looking to Cleito for confirmation. She nodded once.

"Well, I guess this is goodbye, then. It was wonderful to have been here, not only because I found Raif. I'll miss you all." I gave them both hugs, belatedly wondering where Michael was. As if reading my thoughts, he showed up.

"I hope I'm not too late. I think I had one too many drinks in celebration last night." His cheeks flushed.

I hugged him, whispering as quickly and quietly as I could, "Thank you. There are some left on the camera. Can you show him after I've gone?"

"Of course," he mumbled his reply. He picked me up and spun me in a circle playfully before setting me back on my feet. I had to laugh at his free spirit.

Raif was my last goodbye. I looked at him, knowing words would never be enough. My heart was breaking. I desperately wanted to stay with him, but knew it wasn't an option for us. His people needed to surface, mine needed their history, knowledge, and magic, even if we didn't know it. I tried to hold on to the thought that it was only temporary, that someday I'd see him again.

I stood a breath away from him, taking him in one last time. My gaze swept up his strong chest, remembering how safe and comfortable I'd felt in his embrace. I caressed his broad shoulders where I'd placed my head and listened to the rumble of his voice. His beloved face couldn't hide any emotion from me and he was struggling to maintain composure. His captivating teal eyes were swimming with tears that he refused to shed. I knew he'd love me for eternity, as I him. We'd be together again someday. We had to.

"Raif," I whispered. I couldn't get any further as he swept me into his strong embrace, squeezing me as though he couldn't pull me close enough. He gradually released the pressure so I could breathe and stroked his hands up and down my back. They moved up, fisting my hair, forcing my face to tilt and grant him access to administer a passionate kiss. He put all the love he felt for me into that kiss. It was carnal, possessive; a kiss that claimed me as his in every possible way. I kissed him back just as fiercely. I could feel the tears he'd tried to hold back streaming down his cheeks. If I had tears, they'd have mingled with his.

"*My amada, Eu te amo. A miña vida está completa. Ata o dus eu te amo.* My beloved, I love you. My life is complete. I will love you for eternity," I whispered to him in a choked voice in both of our languages. It was more romantic in Atlantean, but I wanted him to know that I understood him from before. He was too choked up to say anything, but I could feel his love in my heart. We'd be linked forever. I had to let go. When I turned, Cleito was weeping and Atreyu and Michael couldn't keep their faces dry. I gave them all a weak smile and walked toward the fountain. Just as I stepped into it, I looked one more time at my *alma xemelga*, my soul's mate. I blew him a kiss and took the final step.

15

I woke with a start. Everything hurt. I felt the grime of the asphalt under my hands and knees when I pushed myself up. I wrapped my arms around my shivering body, unsure and frightened. Steadying myself along a wall, I walked toward the lights and noise I could hear in the distance. I was in an alleyway that opened into a very large shopping district. The shops were starting to close as night descended. I knew I wanted to be inside, I just didn't know where to go. A man wearing a uniform approached me, asking questions I wasn't sure how to answer.

"Miss, are you all right? What is your name? What are you doing here?"

"Igimamablm." My throat hurt like I'd swallowed the gravel I'd woken up on. I cleared my throat and tried again. "Where am I? I think I'm lost." It felt like I'd swallowed a jellyfish, but at least I could speak. I didn't sound like me, but I couldn't completely remember how I was supposed to sound. I felt as if someone had ripped out my heart and replaced it with knives. I just wanted to curl up and die from the intensity of the pain.

"Miss, you're in Bermuda. How'd you get here? Do you have your passport?"

"I don't know how I got here. I don't even know who I am. Bermuda sounds familiar though," I replied, trembling.

"Well, let's get you to the station and into some clean clothes. Beverly should have an extra pair of sweats for you. Can you remember anything?" He asked gently, helping me to stand without the aid of the wall.

"No," I choked out.

I wanted to cry as I clutched his arm but suddenly remembered I didn't have tears. My throat hurt from talking and my head was starting to pound. I wasn't sure where the idea that I could no longer cry came from, but I was certain that it was true. I was also certain that I'd given up my tears for something important.

The officer walked me to the station as I tried desperately to remain upright. My head was starting to hurt as much as my chest. I had the vague sense that I was grieving. I felt a sense of confusion and hurt that didn't necessarily belong to me. I kept this feeling to myself—I imagined that the officer would be more likely to take me to a psych ward than the station if I voiced my thoughts.

The Bermuda Police Station was located on the corner of the pier, so as to keep watch for the tourists both in the shopping square and on the ships. I saw the cruise ship in port and immediately halted.

"Are you all right, miss?" The police officer asked. "Does that look familiar? It just arrived; the passengers should be departing shortly. Maybe you were supposed to be meeting someone?"

"No. I don't live here. All I can remember are teal eyes," I whispered.

I had a sudden case of crippling heartbreak; my knees gave up and I collapsed at the poor officer's feet. I crouched there, my body convulsing in tearless sobs. I could see his face in my memory, but couldn't remember his name. I wept without shedding tears.

"I should've stayed. I should never have come back." I didn't realize I'd spoken out loud until the officer leaned over and stroked my hair whispering words of comfort and encouragement. He looked like he might shed tears for me. He tried to lift me into his arms, but all he managed to do was to wrap me in an embrace and half drag me into the station. There was a man at the counter talking to an older woman. The officer gently put me into one of the most uncomfortable orange chairs I'd ever sat in and turned to talk to the lady behind the desk.

"Beverly, will you please get this poor girl some water and a blanket? I think she's in shock." He came and sat next to me, holding my hand while I tried to pull myself together. I couldn't breathe past the pain and frustration, it was just too much. I forced myself to push the feelings from me with all the strength I could muster, and slowly started to come to myself. I needed to stop having hysterics.

"I'm so sorry. I have no idea what came over me. Thank you." My voice was still scratchy.

"*Tasha?* Is that really you? Oh, thank God you're all right! I saw you hit the tide and you were gone. Oh, baby you're safe." The man from the counter raced over and swept me into his arms. It felt so wrong. The body was shorter and thinner than what I was supposed to have wrapped around me. I had a vivid memory of a very large man's embrace and this was not him.

"Do I know you?" My question startled him as effectively as a blast of icy water to his face. He pulled back so he could study me, which allowed me the same luxury. His blue eyes were red rimmed and haunted. He looked vaguely familiar, and I knew I should find him memorable, but I just couldn't place him.

"Sir, do you know this woman?" The officer stepped in front of me, effectively blocking the man from clutching me to his chest.

"My name is Keith McNamara and this woman is my girlfriend, Natasha James. I came here to report her missing, possibly drowned. We had a scuba diving accident on the ship this afternoon. I thought she'd died. Please, let me look at her." He sounded desperate, his voice thick with hope.

"That was today? I'm sorry," I whispered and shrugged, not remembering enough to continue the thought. I offered them all a small smile, trying to reassure them all that I really wasn't crazy, not fully believing it myself.

"I'm Officer Damon Pendleton, and this woman claims to not have any memory of herself or of anything that happened prior to my finding her in the street. Do you have any proof that she is who you say she is? I also need proof of who you are and your relationship to her in order to let you leave with her." He took this Keith person into the back office to discuss what to do with me.

While they were talking, Beverly found a dry pair of pink Bermuda PD sweats for me to wear. I didn't know much, but I knew I wasn't used to being coddled. Apart from the vague image of a man who I was pretty sure I allowed to coddle me as much as he wanted. I couldn't think about that though, as I was again fighting overwhelming sadness.

"Thank you, Beverly. Where can I change?" I whispered because I couldn't bring myself to talk past the lump forming in my throat. I was a mess.

"Oh, honey. Let's get you into the powder room so you can wash some of the grime off your face. We can put this beautiful dress into a duffle bag for you to wash when you get back home, all right? Come with me, you poor dear." She bustled around me like a grandmother taking care of an ill child. I smiled at the image she conjured in my head. It really was kind of her to help me like she was. I had the vague feeling that kindness didn't always happen in my life.

She led me into the back where there were locker rooms leading into a small gym. We entered the ladies' room, and she had to help me out of my dress and into the shower. As the dress was peeled from me, a small disk plinked onto the floor. My heart leapt at the sight and I knew there were answers on it, if I could just look at it. It was the single most important treasure I possessed on this earth.

"Well now, that's a funny thing to have in your under things. I'll put it in the little pouch here so you don't lose it, okay, honey?" She bustled about as if it were an everyday occurrence to have a naked woman with amnesia in her showers. She helped me to get the worst of the crud off and then helped me into the dry sweats. I felt at least a little more human on the outside. The jury was still out on the rest of me.

"Thanks again, Beverly. I appreciate your kindness more than you know. I wish I knew more about what happened to me, though. This is very frustrating." She patted my cheek and smiled.

"It will come when you're ready, my dear. Come on; let's see what my grandson has figured out. Oops, I mean Officer Pendleton. Don't tell him I slipped." She had a nice rosy tint to her cheeks and I couldn't help the giggle that passed.

"It'll be our secret." I winked at her, enjoying our comfortable banter. I was starting to feel very glad I'd wound up here.

Keith had my identification as well as my information regarding the cruise. He'd planned on reporting me as a missing person and needed that information to submit a report. Now he was arranging things with Officer Pendleton so that we could make it back to the ship without incident. They were having trouble trying to figure out how to get me back onto the cruise ship when I was already reported missing at sea after the dive. They decided that a letter from the police explaining things should be sufficient and were just finishing up.

"Well, you two are free to go. Miss Natasha, you take care of yourself. I sure do hope you find those missing memories." Officer Pendleton shook my hand and I mumbled my thanks. Beverly gave me a great big hug and wished me well. Keith wrapped his arm around my shoulders and walked me out to the ship.

It was a quiet walk, bordering on uncomfortable. I felt like I should say something to him, but didn't know what. His arm was draped possessively across my body and it made me anxious. Distantly, I understood he thought we were romantically involved and having me close was important to him. He wasn't doing anything inappropriate, so I chose to just deal with it.

"You really don't remember anything, do you?" He looked at me with sadness in his eyes and I felt bad.

"I'm really sorry, Keith, but I don't. There are thoughts that keep flitting to the surface, but then they disappear before I can truly grasp them. I see images of eyes, mostly. I feel like I've been in a dream, and am only now waking." We were silent the rest of the way to the ship.

I was nervous about how I was going to be received—it wasn't an everyday occurrence that someone returns from the dead. I hoped they wouldn't make too big a fuss about things. It turns out that my fears were completely unfounded.

My little keycard thing that Keith happened to have with him still worked, so they obviously hadn't closed out my account yet. I wanted to stop by the captain's room to let him know I was still a passenger, and they didn't have a casualty at sea. Keith agreed with me and walked me to the captain's quarters. When the he opened the door, it was obvious that he'd been drinking. We could hear another man's voice in the room behind and knew that we'd interrupted something.

"Sir, I know it's late and I am sorry to disturb you, but I thought it'd be best to let you know that I didn't drown after all. I'm here, and hope that whatever happened didn't cause you too much trouble," I said. I didn't want to linger here. I just wanted to get to my room and pass out for the next few years. My body still ached, my head was pounding, and I was tired of being looked at strangely.

"I'm sorry, who are you?" He swayed slightly and I hoped we wouldn't be shoving off any time soon.

"Her name is Natasha James, she's in room 311, and she was listed as drowned at sea after our dive this afternoon. If you talk to the dive instructor, I believe his name was Jorge Mendoza, he can verify that she was on the dive." Keith saved me from making a complete fool of myself. I hadn't known any of that information. It felt true as he said it, but everything was still just out of reach.

"Tell him yourself. He may still be conscious, poor fellow. I've been trying to get him drunk for the past couple of hours so he can just pass out and forget the whole thing. That man has never lost a body before; he's taking it rather hard." The captain ushered us into his quarters.

The captain was a short, stocky man so he had to move quite a bit out of our way for us to pass him. The entire room reeked of alcohol. Off to the side was a small living area. It boasted a love seat, coffee table, and two reclining chairs. A man was slumped in one of the chairs with an almost completed bottle of whisky dangling precariously from his fingertips.

"Mr. Mendoza? My name is Natasha, and I do believe there was a mix-up earlier today. I was on your dive and must have gotten separated. I'm okay, sir." I gently pried his fingers from around the bottle and tried to get him to look at me.

"Oh, god! She's come to haunt me for my failure!" He was slurring so badly it was difficult to understand him. His eyes were huge and bloodshot, but he was trembling as he looked at me. "Jeff, tell me you see her." The captain came over and placed a comforting hand on his shoulder.

"Jorge, she's not an apparition. This young girl wanted to let you know that she's okay and safely back on board the ship. Perhaps she'll join us for drinks tomorrow when you're more yourself again and explain to us exactly what happened. Sleep now, my friend, your record remains untainted." He placed his other hand comfortingly against the instructor's face, turning him close for an intimate hug.

It was obvious that they were very close in the way that they responded to each other. I was glad that Jorge had Jeff to ease his frustration, and help him to figure out what had happened earlier today. I had a pang of grief for a loss I couldn't remember as Keith took hold of my hand. The grief settled into a now familiar weight of guilt as I realized he thought he was supporting me.

I didn't think it necessary to explain to the captain and diving instructor that I wouldn't be able to tell them what happened because I didn't remember. Maybe I'd remember something if I wasn't so confused. I was starting to become irritable and just wanted to be alone to figure things out. Keith and I said our goodbyes to the two men and he led me to my suite.

It wasn't as opulent as the captain's, but it was cozy. Keith apologized as we walked into the room because he'd packed up my things. I didn't care because at that moment I spotted the bed. I'd never been so tired in all my life. I walked over to it, curled up, and knew that even if he insisted on watching me the whole time, I'd finally find solace in sleep.

"Keith, I'm sorry, but I'm so tired. Can I sleep for a while? I'll try to remember things when I wake, but I'm so tired," I whispered, as I got comfortable.

"Of course. I'm exhausted myself. Is it okay if I stay with you? I feel like I'm dreaming and if I leave, you might not be here when I come back. I won't do anything, I just want to hold you, please." It was the pain in his voice that caused me to cave. I must have been very close to him for him to be so worked up about leaving my room.

"Fine, you can stay, just please be quiet and let me sleep." I drifted off within moments of my head hitting the pillow.

16

I dreamed. They were very strange dreams of things that could not possibly exist. When I woke, the dreams still haunted me. There was death, fighting, and extreme, heartbreaking pain. Underneath the pain, though, was a love and acceptance I couldn't understand. I was still trying to puzzle it all out when Keith walked in.

"Hey, babe! You're finally awake. I was hoping you'd come around soon." At my puzzled expression, he elaborated. "You've been asleep for almost two days. You missed drinks with the captain yesterday. It's the afternoon now. We're leaving port in a few minutes and will be back in Miami tomorrow. There've been some people asking about you. Do you feel up to going to a late lunch or early dinner with me?"

"I don't know what good it'll do, I don't remember anything. I am hungry, though." He smiled at me as if I'd just proven the existence of Santa. My guilt returned at not knowing this man who I must have once had a deep affection for. "Give me half an hour to shower and change." I fell out of bed and staggered to the bathroom. He tried to help, but at my glare decided to sit on the bed and wait quietly.

The shower was glorious. I couldn't remember the last time a shower felt so good, and then started laughing because I couldn't remember much of anything at all. The bathroom was steamy when I got out, sending another flicker of a memory to my addled brain. The last time I'd bathed, there hadn't been any steam. I'd been in an elegant bath preparing for something important. I still couldn't catch the thread of memory to place what it was, but I knew it had been an event that changed my world forever. The more I struggled for the memory the more elusive it became, and I was quickly frustrated. I threw the towel on the ground with more force than necessary and ran a brush through my hair, trying to eliminate my growing aggravation as easily as I removed the tangles.

I sighed, grumbling to myself as I went into the bedroom to get dressed. I froze. I'd completely forgotten about Keith. His jaw dropped, and the smell of lust quickly filled the air. I dimly thought about how strange it was to actually smell lust as I grabbed the first thing I could find and wrapped it around me. He groaned, closing his eyes. I looked down to see that I'd covered myself with one of my sheer sarongs. My body was still completely on display, but in a much more sensual way.

"I'm so sorry, Keith. I totally forgot you were still here. I didn't mean to—" He cut me off with a wave of his hand.

"Don't worry about it. Please, just get dressed, unless you've changed your mind. We could just order room service and stay here." Thankfully his eyes were still shut so he didn't see the shudder I couldn't repress. It wasn't that I didn't like him, but he just wasn't Raif. My heart stuttered.

"Raif! That's it! Do you know that name?" I asked excitedly, finally remembering something important.

"Um, no. Did you remember something? Are you decent yet, or are we having sex? My control isn't that great when it comes to you." He sat rigidly on the bed with his hand still covering his eyes. His other hand was clutching at the blanket so hard I thought it might rip.

"Oops, sorry. I'm not sure, just the name; Raif. Maybe it's reef? This is so frustrating!" Everything felt like it was just out of reach. "Give me another minute." I quickly put on my swimsuit, a solid red sarong, and a black top. I looked presentable and told him so. He pulled himself together and led me out of the room.

I couldn't remember what types of food I liked, so Keith thought that going to the buffet would be an effective way for me to try a little of everything. On our way there, a man came barreling toward me and folded me into a fierce bear hug. He was screeching like a banshee as he squeezed the life out of me. He smelled musky, like freshly turned earth after a storm. Underneath that smell was something different, something I couldn't quite place and didn't have the opportunity to as he pulled away to talk to me.

"Oh, girl! We thought we lost you. Don't you ever do that to us again. Keith told us about your memory, so I'm Maurice, and this hot stud is Stuart. He's mine, so don't go getting any ideas." He laughed at his joke, winking at me, and I couldn't help smiling back. His excitement was infectious, even if I couldn't place him. "We met you here on the ship, and just adore you. Your memory will come back, honey, I just know it. Do you have any memories at all?" He held me at arm's length, tears filling his eyes as I answered.

"Nope, sorry. I get bits and pieces, but mostly it's all a blank." I shrugged, feigning a nonchalance I didn't feel and smiled at him reassuringly. His eyes threatened to spill over as he pulled me into another hug.

"Well now, don't you worry about anything, it'll come back, if only so you can tell me all about what happened. Almost lost at sea! Stuart, I do believe this has been the most exciting vacation we've ever had. Couldn't you just die?" Stuart grabbed him by the waist giving me a tight-lipped smile.

"Sorry, he just gets a little excited. We are both very glad that you are safe." He gave me a small hug and I caught a whiff of his deep, earthy smell. It was the same scent covering Maurice's, but much stronger.

My stomach growled and I laughed. We made our way to the buffet to fill our plates. Maurice thought Keith was brilliant to have thought about the buffet to help jog some memories for me and decided he'd try everything along with me. We were lucky to have gotten the big table as we had two of everything the buffet held, plus food for Stuart and Keith.

I had an absolute blast eating a bit of everything with Maurice. He about fell out of his chair laughing at me when I attempted to eat seafood; the expression of disgust on my face was too much for him. Stuart and Keith kept to themselves mostly; joining in on some of the laughter, but mostly just watching us like parents watch their unruly children. We ate, laughed, and drank until the sun started to color the horizon. I was enjoying myself but couldn't suppress the urge to go up on deck to watch the sunset on the water.

I excused myself from the group, wanting nothing more than to be alone. I made my way to the pool and sat on one of the seats along the deck. The sunset was beautiful, but not as beautiful as the last sunset that I'd seen. I felt the memory tug at my subconscious and rather than struggle for it, I tried to relax and let it come back on its own.

The clouds couldn't hide the luminescent sphere protecting us from the miles of ocean water that pressed against it. The flickers of light twinkled as the bioluminescent fish moved above. It looked like strangely shaped fireflies dancing above our heads. Only, there were dozens of them, and some were larger than any fish I'd ever seen in person. The sphere was illuminated to the west, mimicking the sunset I knew couldn't really appear this far below the ocean's surface. I could feel strong arms encircling me, making me feel tiny, protected, and deeply loved. The body behind me trembled, in desire or despair. I turned to hold him close to me. I glimpsed his face and remembered everything about him. Raif. My soul's mate, my other half, the piece of myself I wasn't certain I'd ever see again.

I sat up rigidly in my seat, pale and trembling. I remembered. Everything. I finally understood the grief I could still feel flooding through me, breaking my heart continuously. I now knew why I couldn't cry, although I desperately needed to at this moment. I felt arms start to tentatively slide around my waist and for one glorious moment I thought Raif was here. I leaned into the embrace, turning to reciprocate and gasped.

"No!" I breathed out a pain filled denial in Keith's face, pushing him away from me. I knew my expression was one of crushed sorrow and felt bad knowing that he'd misunderstand the depth of my negative response. I watched in agony as he battled with the rejection. He failed miserably, crumbling into helpless tears on one of the seats.

"Keith, I'm so sorry." I dropped to his side, silently stroking his back. I didn't know what else to say to him. Anything I could think of would just hurt him further and I didn't want to do that after everything he'd done for me. I felt like a horrible person. He was mumbling something I could barely understand. "What do you need? Can I get or do anything for you? God, I'm so sorry."

"Leave. Please just leave," he whispered between his tears. I left, but didn't go too far. Perhaps it was better this way. He'd be able to forget about me and find his mate, as he should. I was grateful to have my memory back, but I wasn't quite sure what to do now. I couldn't very well go back home with Keith when I was married to another man. I shuddered to think of what would've eventually happened if I'd been unable to retrieve my memories. I just wished someone would tell me what was supposed to happen next.

The pool deck was divided into two sections. The pool I'd just vacated being on the uppermost portion of the deck. I was currently making my way along the lower half of the deck, not wanting to completely abandon Keith to his frustrations but also needing to leave him alone for a while.

I was thinking about Raif, when suddenly a familiar smell washed over me. A very strong cologne masked Stuart's base scent, but he still smelled earthy. I'd been noticing that I was able to smell and hear things much more clearly than I had before, but still didn't completely understand why. My lips curved into a slight smile in greeting as I turned to Stuart.

"I saw Keith. He seems miserable. What happened?" He was showing a gentle, fatherly concern for me as he had throughout the entire trip. Underneath his concern, though, I thought I could hear a very controlled tone of anticipation.

"I remembered things, but that isn't what upset him. I rejected him again. I've been doing it since I got back and I think it's been too much for him. He seems to care a great deal about me." I wanted to explain myself, tell him why I continued to reject Keith, but I couldn't. I wanted to shout to everyone that I was already mated, loved, and accepted by my soul mate, but I couldn't. I tried to form the words, but they wouldn't come out. I cleared my throat and attempted again to launch into the whole story for Stuart, but it was as if the words dried up in my throat before I could speak them. This was an odd turn of events. I wondered if I'd ever be able to tell anyone what had happened, or if this was part of the magic that is Atlantis—a spell to protect them.

"Keith does love you. That much has been obvious every time Maurice and I have seen you together. Maurice is already planning our trip for your eventual wedding. You made quite an impression on him." Stuart smiled as he settled himself against the railing beside me. He casually leaned against it, watching the last of the sun's rays disappear beneath the waves.

"You have both been wonderful. I feel as if I've known you forever, not just the few days of this trip. I'd love to see you if you two ever decide to visit," I replied absentmindedly. "Oh, good. He's going back to his room." I visibly relaxed against the railing knowing that Keith wasn't going to do something stupid. I looked over to see Stuart eyeing me strangely.

"How did you know that? We cannot see him from here." He couldn't fully contain the suspicious glee from his voice.

"I heard him, didn't you?" I tried to mask my feelings. "Where's Maurice? I thought you two went everywhere together." If I hadn't been watching, I'd have missed the barely suppressed shudder. My pulse increased as I realized that something wasn't right. I unexpectedly felt off balance. I wasn't sure if it was too much wine, or the recent emotional turmoil from the invasion of my memories, but suddenly I felt awful.

"He is sleeping off some of the wine. I wanted to see the sunset before I retired. Did you know that this is the exact spot where we lost you?" He turned to gaze at the water as he talked. I was having a difficult time following what he was saying. I got a fresh whiff of his cologne and felt dizzy, the smell making me nauseous.

"Really? I didn't know that. I'm sorry, Stuart, I think I ate something that doesn't agree with me. I have to go lay down." I took a step to leave and he grabbed my arm in a vise-like grip.

"You are mated," he growled in my ear. "I could smell it the first time I saw you after Bimini. I was supposed to go home, but you had to go and get yourself mated. You bitch." He spun me so I could see the barely contained anger swirling in the depths of his multi-hued brown eyes. I let out a startled gasp as I realized that he was from Atlantis.

"H-how is this possible? How'd you get up here? Is Raif here?" I asked, hopefully, knowing that if he were, I'd have felt it.

"Raif? You must mean Raifuku. He mated with you?" His disgust was palpable. "It's no matter. You now have Atlantean blood running through your veins and must die." He started pulling me toward the railing. I started struggling through the haze in my brain. Why was it so foggy?

"What'd you do to me?" I didn't really expect an answer, so I was surprised when he responded.

"It is the way this cologne mixes with my natural aura. I discovered by accident that the smell causes other Atlanteans not of my clan to become violently ill. Victoria is still sleeping off the effects it had on her. Although, her blood is richer than yours; I was taking a risk assuming it would work on you. I believe it was a well-played risk."

I wanted to punch the smug expression off his face. I couldn't believe Raif had wanted to save these people. They were constantly talking about, or actively trying, to kill me.

"What about Maurice? Is he sleeping off the drug, too?" I tried to distract him since he seemed willing to talk to me. My vision started to blur and I knew that I had to keep him distracted until someone came on deck or I figured out how to escape. I couldn't fight him and win.

"No, I slipped a few sleeping pills into his port. He should sleep until we arrive in Miami. He was a fun toy, but has served his purpose. I'll be taking you with me back to Atlantis, and finally be welcomed to my home like the prince I am!" As he gloated I brought my foot up to his groin, kicking him with all I had.

He fell to the ground, groaning in pain. I was distantly relieved to know that Maurice was well, but concerned about Victoria. To think, she was from Atlantis as well! I pushed those thoughts from my head as I ran away from him. It was more of a drunken stagger, but I managed to make it through most of the chairs on deck before he grabbed me. I could see the stairs just a few feet ahead and I screamed for help. It was hoarser than I'd intended, but all I needed was one more person on the deck. I thrashed, twisted, and desperately tried to fight him through the fog that was my brain. It was a struggle just to stay conscious.

I saw the railing again in my peripheral and I forced my limbs to do something. The fog was coming faster the closer I was to his body as all I could smell was him. It wasn't as if I didn't want to go back to Atlantis, but there was no way of knowing for sure that we would. I really didn't want to die now that I'd found my soul mate. I prayed for a miracle.

She came with disheveled hair and frumpy clothing, brandishing a very large metal pipe. I ducked just as she swung, and heard a massive, juicy thwack behind me. I fell to the ground tangled with Stuart and covered with his blood, brains, and pieces of his skull.

"Asshole! How could you drug your own kind?" Her voice shrilled in anger. "Are you all right, Natasha?" I looked up at Victoria in all her brilliant rage and thought I was looking at an angel. It was the most I'd ever heard her speak, and the worst I'd ever seen her look, but she was beautiful.

"I think so. Will you help me up? I honestly don't know how I'm even still conscious." I lifted a gore-splattered hand, trying desperately not to think about the brains on my arms as she lifted me up. She sniffed my neck as she pulled me close.

"So, it's true," she said in awe, her expression mystified. "My master thought you might be the one, but he wasn't sure. He sent me here to watch and protect you, if necessary. It was fortunate for you that Stuart attacked during the night, as I'm mostly useless during the day. Add that stupid drug to the mix and let's just say that you are one lucky girl. You need to go get cleaned up somewhere where no one will see you. I'll clean this up." She gestured to the body still on deck. "Don't speak of this to anyone. I'll find you later." With that, she lifted Stuart's body as if he was nothing but a bag of flour and tossed him overboard. She removed her shirt to clean the deck, and I ran to my suite.

17

We arrived in Miami without any further incidents. No one noticed Stuart was missing until Maurice woke two hours before arriving in the Miami port. It was chaos as people looked around for the missing passenger. Maurice was devastated and I didn't have the heart to tell him what had happened. Not that I could have even if I'd wanted to, he was surrounded by people. He was a very popular man, especially with a certain male crowd. Somehow, I knew he'd eventually be okay.

"I'm still going to come back with you, if that's okay." Keith's voice intruded on my musings, mumbling something about his parents.

"I'm sorry things turned out how they did, Keith," I replied, hoping he could hear the sincerity in my voice. "I do care about you, and I hope we can be friends." Disappointment flashed across his face, and I knew that friendship between us would never exist. He believed he loved me, and while I truly cared for him, I could never love him as I did Raif.

"Of course. I'll see you on the plane," he replied, rushing off to meet back up with his friends before our departure from the ship. I secretly wondered how many other friendships I'd lose from this trip. It had started out so promising, but was ending with such heartbreak; it was hard to not be depressed. I held onto the flicker of life I could feel in my heart. Knowing that Raif was out there, waiting for me, kept me going.

Victoria met me on the docks. She hadn't said anything to me since Stuart's death the night before and for that I was grateful. It was not a night I wanted to remember. It was hard to believe that less than a week had passed since I'd boarded the ship. With all that had happened, I felt like years had gone by.

"You will come with me. Everything will be explained once we reach my master. Come." Every inch of her was covered. Huge, dark tinted glasses covered half her face, while a scarf covered her mouth, obscuring any facial expression.

She had been dressed in a very similar manor when we'd gone diving. For someone so young, she really didn't like the sun. I didn't have anything pressing, and I was curious to know who'd sent her, so I followed her. We flagged a cab and I was surprised when we pulled up to the Krypt Keeper.

"Why are we going to a bar? I thought we had to meet your boss?" I was feeling uneasy about having gotten into a cab with someone who was essentially a stranger.

"We are. Come." She got out of the cab and walked into the club as if she owned the place. I supposed I could have just asked the cabbie to take me somewhere else, anywhere else but here, but I felt that I owed her and her boss for protecting me.

The bar was much less magnificent during the day. The strobes were off, as were all the colored lights. It was still dimly lit; the only patrons sitting at the bar were drinking and watching the news before they headed home. I could smell their desperation to be free of their lives of monotony.

The men barely paid any attention to me or to Victoria, who'd begun to shed her many layers. She was down to a low-cut halter, snug, low-rise jeans, and black sling backs. She shook out her blonde hair, pushing her glasses on top of her head to reveal a bright red sunburn line that dissipated before my eyes.

"Natasha, how good of you to visit again. I trust your vacation went well?" Stephan glided toward me, embracing me in a friendly hug. He was still magnificent with his molten silver eyes accented by just a hint of coal. I hugged him back.

"It was eventful. Victoria and I are here to meet her boss so I can thank him for sending her to watch out for me. She was a life-saver." He bowed, giving me his arm as he stood to walk me over to Victoria.

"Master," she said bitterly as way of greeting, bowing low to kiss his hand. "I brought her back safely, just as you requested. There was one of the Earthen on board that was disposed of. He'd found a way to incapacitate the other clans. We'll have to be more proactive in the future. I was not expecting an attack from one of our own. I hunger, and must rest. This has been a most unpleasant task for me. Do I have your leave?"

"Feed and sleep. We will talk of this attack tomorrow night. You've done well, Victoria." Just before she ran off to the back hall I saw her slight smile of appreciation. It transformed her from pretty to breathtaking.

"So, you're her boss? No offense, but why would a bar owner be interested in my welfare?" I appraised Stephan coolly. I casually removed my arm, standing across from him in a defensive posture.

"You may have already noticed that Victoria is not all that she seems to be. Neither am I. This club is not just a bar, either. I created this place to be a haven for the other Atlanteans that were trapped here after the island sank. I, myself, am from Atlantis." He waited for me to grasp that knowledge and ordered us both drinks. I sat in stunned silence for a few minutes in the nearest chair, digesting the fact that not only had I visited a mythical country, but its inhabitants had also been living in our society for thousands of years without our knowledge.

"Please, go on. How'd you know my name before? Why'd you send Victoria? What's going to happen to me now?" I was proud that my voice didn't tremble.

"Lady Natasha, I intend you no harm. I was once Poseidon's high priest sent with the troops to enlist Poseidon's guidance during our plunder. It was a massive failure, as you know. We did not know that Atlantis had sunk until we tried to return, empty-handed. Our people were not welcomed into any other nation, so we drifted at sea. Poseidon would not answer my prayers for weeks, as he was so grieved by the betrayal of his kin and the loss of his mate. When he finally did answer, he was merely a shadow of the god he once was. He decreed that until Atlantis rose again and we had access to the healing waters, we'd live on the blood of our fellow man. It was our bloodshed that got us into this mess, so with bloodshed we would be forced to continue our existence."

"Wow. So, what, you drink the blood of others to survive?" It was hard to miss the sarcasm in my voice. I downed my drink and put it back on the bar. Vampires. It was too much. I quietly remembered the kiss we'd shared before I left on the cruise. How he'd sucked on my neck in what I'd thought was an attempt to leave a hickey. I thought of Victoria's sunburn from the few minutes we were out in the sun earlier, and started to tremble with real fear. "Are you trying to tell me that you and every Atlantean remaining on the surface are vampires? How could Victoria be out during the day if she is one of the bloodsucking horde?"

"Not all of us are vampires. The one you met on the ship was a member of a different clan, and therefore was destined to follow a different path than Victoria and me. Victoria can still withstand a bit of sunlight to an extent, as she is not wholly Atlantean and still a relatively young vampire. The history of my kin is not pleasant.

"Very few of us survived our initial mission, even fewer wanted to live on blood for all of eternity. The idea of being immortal, surprisingly, does not appeal to everyone. Most of us had lost loved ones; families slaughtered by Poseidon's rage, or they had succumbed to the anger of the other gods' wrath. It was not just Zeus that we'd angered with our prideful arrogance, and most were not content to leave us exiled. I left behind a younger brother, who is now Poseidon's new high priest."

"I met him. He was interesting." It was the kindest thing I could have said. I thought about Atreyu and finally noticed the similarities between him and Stephan. The silver undertone of Stephan's skin was slighter than Atreyu's, but it was there now that I was looking for it. Their eyes were the same silver, and while Stephan had short, dark hair, he also had three thin braids woven in, but tucked away. While I could see a family resemblance, there was a distinct difference in their personalities. Atreyu had a power and vibrancy to him, while Stephan just seemed sad and worn.

Stephan nodded, continuing as if I hadn't even spoken. "Life, as we had been accustomed to, no longer existed for us. We were outcasts. Poseidon guided us to this unclaimed land and here we have lived for over eleven thousand years. Of the one hundred twenty of us left from the failed plunder, only twenty remain in existence today."

"What happened?" Lines appeared across his skin for a brief second, pain of thousands of years showing for a moment before disappearing. I almost regretted my question.

"That is not a story you need to hear just yet. Just know that while my people were excellent warriors, there was a limit to the amount of bloodshed even we could live with. Those of us that remain have had to learn to deal with the death we have caused."

"Do you have to kill each time you feed?" I could barely hear my own voice, I wasn't certain I wanted to know that answer. I liked Stephan. I didn't want to know that he killed nightly to survive.

"No. There was a time when we didn't know this, but we now mostly live off donors and excess blood from blood banks. There are also people who think they know about us, but believe we're figments of their fantasies. They come to the clubs to feed us."

I was at a loss for words. My disbelief and anger quickly faded with the intensity of his pain. His story was filled with loss and grief. I didn't want him to continue, but there was still so much I wanted to know. There'd been too much heartache in recent days, I just couldn't add to it. My questions could wait. I had a lifetime to figure out my new family, I didn't have to peel the Band-Aid away so quickly.

"So, why a bar?"

"Excuse me?" He looked up at me, trying to gather control.

"You've been here for quite a while, so why a bar? Why even work at all? I'm sure you're loaded. You should be, for living as long as you have. I'm curious as to why you'd choose to own a bar." He looked at me for a few minutes gauging the sincerity in my change of subject.

"I like human interaction," he finally said. I knew there was more, so I leaned back with an eyebrow raised, waiting for him to continue. "With my affliction, it's easier to find willing donors in a public place where people are comfortable and slightly inebriated. This is also a haven for those that share the Atlantean bloodline. I am sure you're aware that we all possess gifts of some kind?" I nodded. "Well, some handle it better than others. We also have discovered, quite by accident, that these gifts can occasionally be given to others. There are other places like this bar, set up by the remaining twenty. Here we can come and be accepted for the things that make us different. Here we cannot be hunted. Here we are welcomed, loved, and free." I had thought to lighten the mood, but he was insisting on bringing things down.

"So, Victoria is one that you shared your gift with?"

"No, Victoria's maker was cruel. The madness of being away from our people finally controlled his mind completely. He made dozens of half-breeds before he was stopped. I inherited most of them, as I am the oldest and strongest of us all. Victoria was one of the few that showed promise. It's her choice to tell you of what happened, just know that she shares my hopes for the future."

"What am I supposed to do now?"

"Whatever you wish, but know that you are always welcome here. We will train you as we try to protect you, or you can go back to your people and wait for Atlantis to rise. Whatever you choose, you must know that you cannot speak of Atlantis to anyone who has not been there or does not share one of our gifts. It is part of the curse of us being on the surface.

"Being alone here is difficult. If you decide that it is too burdensome, know that you will always have a home here. May the gods bless you with clear skies and strong winds at your back." With those parting words he stood, gathered me in an embrace, and left me to decide what I wanted to do.

Without a clear idea of what I should do, or where I should go, I made my way back to my hotel room. Of all the things I didn't know, one thing was clear. My life was completely different now. I already had enhanced vision and hearing, who knew what else might happen. Was I now considered a pure blood because I was mated to an Atlantean warrior? Would I be able to change too? Would the constant ache in my chest ever diminish? I wondered for the thousandth time what Raif was doing, and when we'd be together again.

18

Keith was happy during the whole flight, chatting about all the things we would do when we got back. It had been years since he'd been back to see his family and it appeared he was really going to try to give this friendship thing a shot. I tried to share his enthusiasm. It was difficult to be excited with him because I still wasn't sure what I was going to do when I got home. All I knew was I was very excited to see Ashlyn and Katie—I missed them both terribly.

I also wasn't feeling very well. I'd woken up feeling distracted and not like myself. I half-listened to Keith's rant about the changes he was going to make to his parent's company as I tried to pinpoint exactly why I felt so strange.

"It's gone!" I hadn't meant to exclaim out loud.

"What's gone? Did you lose the bracelet I gave you? I can get you another one if you want." He grabbed my hand to see. I snatched it away, not wanting him to notice that I was still wearing my wedding band.

"No, I still have that. I put it on the other wrist, see?" I showed him my right hand where the little silver bracelet shone on my wrist. "I've been having a weird sense of misery lately, and I just realized that when I woke up this morning, it was gone. I feel at peace, it's wonderful."

We smiled at each other. I was happy to finally feel peace again, and Keith thought I was finally getting over my issues. I let him think whatever he wanted as long as he was happy. He still had my hand in his and was caressing it with his thumb. Between that soft caress, his quiet, happy aura, and the fact that I wasn't radiating pain at the moment, I was able to sleep the whole flight home. When I woke, I was still feeling off, but it was different. It wasn't Raif I was feeling, but my own unease.

Katie and Ashlyn were waiting for me at baggage claim. Ash was holding a bear as big as her with a big sign that said, "Welcome Home, Aunt Tash!" It was written with every color crayon in her crayon box except orange. Ash hated orange. I smiled as I saw them. If I had to be without my mate, life couldn't be sweeter than to be with them. I ran up to Ashlyn, scooping her and the bear into a giant hug and tickled her side. She smelled of innocence and home and I couldn't help but smile at her.

"Aunt Tash, stop!" she squealed. I settled her against my hip.

"Hey, booger, I missed you," I said as I squeezed her again. "I think you grew another three feet while I was gone."

"Nope, but I made you a poster and Bear wanted to hold it. He missed your lame stories. I told him we'd have a good one tonight, just like you promised. He wanted to make sure you were really coming home. Who's that?" She pointed over my shoulder to Keith. I'd hoped he'd give me some time with my family, but apparently not. I had no idea how to introduce her to him, as he wasn't what he wanted to be with me and never would be.

"This is my friend, Keith. Your mom and I were friends with him before you were born and I ran into him on the ship. Hey, Katie, you remember Keith, right?" I glanced over to Katie who was pale and visibly trembling. I could tell she was trying to get herself under control, but couldn't figure out the cause to her extreme reaction. I turned to her and gathered her into my free arm. Together, Ash and I hugged Katie. We were all smiling, even if Katie's was a bit forced. I was happy our little family was complete again.

Keith said hello to them and made an excuse to leave, promising to see me sometime later. He surprised me by giving me a kiss on my cheek just before he walked off. Ash thought this was fantastic. She teased me about cooties and kissing in trees for the entire ride home. Katie was uncharacteristically silent.

"I picked up a shift and have to work tonight. Are you okay with watching Ash?" she asked abruptly as we walked through the door.

"Sure, I just thought we'd do something together tonight, I haven't seen either of you in a week. Are you okay?" I asked.

"Just tired. I'm glad you're home, though. We'll talk tomorrow, okay?" With that she turned and walked to her room. I was very leery as I watched her leave.

"Okay, Ash, it's just you and me tonight. What do you want for dinner?"

"Ice cream. The good stuff that they make on those stone things. Mom's been making me eat healthy all week. It's gross. Where's my stuff?" She demanded, arms on hips.

"My goodness, I'm home a whole two minutes and you are already demanding things." I comically placed the back of my hand on my forehead and rolled it as I bowed to her. "Your highness, please forgive me."

She laughed, running from me, as she knew the routine. I chased her around the living room before tackling her. I had her pinned with her shirt pulled to expose her belly and she screeched in anticipation.

"Shh. Your mom is trying to sleep." I said in a loud whisper with a big grin on my face. I lowered my head to her belly and blew raspberries until her shrieking giggles became too loud.

She helped me unpack while her mom slept. I gave her the cotton dresses I'd found, the sarong pants I knew she'd find just crazy enough to love, and the seashell jewelry. She spent a few hours quietly looking at all the stuff I'd collected for her and her mom while I relaxed. It was peaceful; although I couldn't remember a time I'd been more exhausted. I found myself dozing on and off while Ash played with her treasures. Neither one of us realized that Katie had left for work until she'd been gone for an hour. I was really concerned, as she'd never left the house without saying goodbye to us.

"Did something happen with your mom this week, Ash?"

"Nope. We went to the zoo, and up to Tahoe to go swimming. She's fine. Are you gonna take me for ice cream? I'm starving." She bounced out of the room with more energy than one person should ever have, leaving me with no choice but to follow.

"AUNT TASH, will you tell me a story? I can't sleep."

"Of course you can't, you ate about five pounds of ice cream. Do you want one of your books?" I grinned at her as I got up from the couch to follow her to her room.

"No, one of your stories," she said as she wiggled under the covers with Bear next to her.

"I thought you hated my stories," I said as I snuggled next to her in my story seat.

"You promised to have a good one made up when you got back. You're back now and Bear wants a story. You owe me, and it had better be good!" She crossed her arms in a mock pout and I couldn't help but laugh at her. I reached over and tickled her. She was a balm to my frayed existence. I decided I'd try to tell her about soul mates.

"All right, settle down. Ready?" At her eager nod, I smiled and curled up next to her. I snuggled her protectively under my arm while I talked and stroked her hair. She closed her eyes and listened. It was our tradition, and one I was glad to resume.

"Once upon a time, there was a soul. It was happy and content to play in the spray of water from a fountain, reflecting light into rainbows. It had never known pain, or sadness, only joy and contentment. This soul was pure, innocent, and full of love. One day an evil wizard came by and watched the soul. He was so jealous of its happiness that he contrived a spell that tore the soul in half. The wizard thought that the soul should know the pain of the loneliness that he felt, and it would amuse him to place the two pieces of soul into two separate beings.

"One piece was placed into a beautiful young princess, and the other was put into a handsome farmer on a magical island. Years went by, and the soul learned sadness. The princess felt like she was missing something, but didn't know what it was. She was very sad and lonely, despite being surrounded by people who loved and cherished her. She'd heard stories about soul mates, and how if you find yours, you're whole again, and she wished for that on the evening star every night. Her father had arranged for her to marry a duke, so she knew time was running out to find her soul's other half.

"The night before the wedding was supposed to take place, the princess was making her wish. So intent was she in wishing to find her soul mate, she didn't hear the intruder until it was too late. She was captured and taken to a magical hidden island by a very bad man. He was an evil prince who wanted the beautiful princess all to himself. He'd heard of her beauty and thought he deserved to have the most beautiful princess as his bride. He was a very selfish man.

"The princess was very cunning, a trait that she hid behind her beauty. She outsmarted the evil prince and managed to escape his castle. She found her way to a small farm, deciding to hide herself in the hayfield until the evil prince passed by. The farmer was tending to his flock when he saw the girl trying to hide in his field. The moment their eyes met, their souls recognized each other and melded to become one again. The broken soul was happy for the first time since the evil wizard played his horrible trick.

"Alas, in a cruel twist of fate, the princess was not allowed to stay on the island. For if she was found, the selfish prince would kill her and her mate. Her mate couldn't return with her to her lands because there was powerful magic that prevented people who were born on the island from ever leaving. Because she was not born there, she could leave, knowing that her soul mate was safe and protected.

"With a heavy heart, she made the decision to leave and made her way back to her land. She married the duke that her father wanted her to, thereby destroying the hopes of the selfish prince. She lived out her days as happy as she was able to be, hoping that someday it would be safe for her to return to her soul mate." I kissed Ashlyn on the forehead as I finished the story. I hadn't really meant to tell her that story. I'd wanted it to be happy so that she'd want to find her mate. She'd been quiet for quite a while, and I hoped that she had fallen asleep. I started to slide out of her room when she spoke.

"Aunt Tash?"

"Yeah, sugar?"

"That story still sucked. It wasn't a very happy story at all. Fairy tales are supposed to have happy endings. You must miss Reef really bad."

"Who?" My heart skipped a beat. How on earth did she know about him? I hadn't been able to talk about him to anyone since I'd gotten back. I barely heard her response over the thudding in my chest.